I0841206

GIRL UNRESERVED

TASHIA HART

NOT TOO FAR REMOVED PRESS

OTHER BOOKS BY TASHIA HART

Native Love Jams (2023)

The Good Berry Cookbook: Harvesting and Cooking Wild Rice and Other Wild Foods (2021)

Gidjie and the Wolves (2020)

Girl Unreserved (2015)

CONTENTS

1

EIGHT

MY NAME IS WINNOW Sticks, and I'm from the Red Lake Nation of Chippewa Indians in Northern Minnesota.

But don't get too excited. I'm not like a real Indian or anything. I don't have any papers that say I'm an *official* Indian.

My face,
an unenrolled identity.
My bloodlines,
the tributaries of a river that gather
the run-off of millenia
of nations amassed.
My identity
an estuary,
before an endless wave of skin.

My skin is so big, it fills up the universe. It's a little known secret, but my skin is what scientists call "the fabric of space-time." But it's not really my skin. I didn't make it and I don't know who did. I'm just gathering some of it for a lifetime.

My gramma tells me that identity is young, but skin is old. She says our identities come into focus where story runs through skin like water drawn through a faucet. She says skin's the stuff we're made of, the stuff that gets recycled over and over again but never forgets where it's been because of the storywater that's always flowing through it.

Storywater is alive you see, and it's movement, although it runs through us all, we feel it separately where our individual flavors of briny sweat, blood, and tears bead up from our skin as context sieved out of a mystery.

The biggest stories are easier to tell in smaller quantities. Our eyes, ears, heart, mind, tongue and hands are the tools we use to gather the skin and create passageways for the storywater to flow into our lives in just the right quantities. How we use these tools to gather our story makes all the difference in how we identify with the water, our skin, and everything else.

Gramma says many people have forgotten how to use their tools, and so have forgotten the gifts of the storywaters. She says eyes look through them, ears ignore them, hearts close off to them, mind discredits them, tongue speaks not of them, and hands, well gramma says that hands try to tear them apart. Even so, she says, every person on Earth—every person in the *universe* comes from a long line of story gatherers whether they know it or not.

Sometimes gramma talks about her own body as if it has characteristics other than those I see and know her to possess: the shortest adult in our family, with dark brown, tree bark-colored skin; her hair died black but white at the roots, always either in curlers or fresh out of curlers; polyester button down shirts and matching straight-leg polyester slacks; and I think gramma's slippers might be permanently affixed to her feet. This is how I see my grandmother.

But if you ask her, she'll tell you all that stuff is but one layer of her embodiment.

She says that the universe dreams and so we dream, and that our dream bodies are one and the same with the universe's body of dreams. She says the dream body does not fit neatly into our physical bodies, and it can feel as though each of these bodies has its own space and dimension that feels like home when you're there.

She says she can see stories in her bodies that are also gathered into mine, or a bird's, or a tree's, or even the sky, and that these stories, these *movements* are gathered more tightly in some places than others.

Where there is much tightness, gramma says that movements begin to slow down and start looking like *things*. And *things* can be plucked from the movement with our minds and held onto, or shared with others, for better or worse. She says you can know people and animals and spirits in this way, by understanding what kinds of things they carry, how they carry them, and when and if they're willing to let them go.

Gramma says the more *things* you gather, the less room there is for the movement of storywater in your life, and that madness is born in the deserts of our minds.

She says we are supposed to help each other let go of things so we can widen our waters and recognize our relation to one another and be full.

Unlike my gramma, some of the Indians around here tell me that because I have no Indian name, the spirits don't know I'm a real thing. And because I don't speak to the spirits in our language, they don't understand what I'm saying.

To that, I say the spirits are crafty, and have come to understand the motion of my gathering tongue, even if it means they've had to fashion a hearing aid out of the spirit of translation herself.

But that's just a silly idea I tell myself to feel better after ducking a drunken verbal assault by my uncle on everyone and everything.

My uncle is full of ideas about men and women, and as I know too well, ideas about children. Children should be seen not heard, which for my uncle means that when he comes home drunk to my gramma's house, he takes off his boots and throws them at us if we're in the same room as him, playing or giggling.

One time his boot caught my sister Maggie upside the head and she had a bloody-looking eye for about a week. We told my parents on him, of course, but he was an adult and my parents seem to think everything we tell them is make believe. It's frustrating.

Sometimes when they refuse to listen to me, I will go in my room and cry to my stuffed dog and tell him all of my problems. And all of my secrets. And ask him all of my heart's questions. I wipe my tears on his eyes and pretend he is crying because he understands what I'm going through.

Anyway, I don't let other people's ideas about me get to me. I know the movement through my skin is bigger than ideas and needs a gathering tongue to tell its ever widening tale.

There are many descriptions for me, depending on what truth of tongue you use, but tell you my truth, the only shape of identity that has begun to come into focus is the movement of me being a girl.

About Being a Girl

I would've been named Winona, but my cousin was also born in 1981, and was given the name just days before I was born. Mom says the name comes from the Sioux, and means "first born daughter." I told mom that didn't make sense, seeing as how I was her second daughter, but mom said that I was born alone, I'd die alone (which, hearing at five years old was a bit much), and so

I had earned the right to be called first born just like any other.

My cousin Winona is half Mexican. Her dad is my dad's brother. He's from Red Lake too. She's lived in Los Angeles her whole life. Her dad moved there in 1968 when my grandparents separated and grampa split for the west coast with two little boys in toe. My dad, his older brother Mitchell, and their sister Shelly stayed with Gramma on the reservation.

Winona and I both have long black hair and brown eyes. But I have freckles. Lots of freckles. She's darker skinned than I am, but daddy says that's mostly from the California sun. I get the feeling dad tries to make me feel better about not having darker skin, but I'm fine with it. I love my skin. And I love my white momma.

Anyways, bent on keeping the name, my mother decided to change it just different enough for it to be our own. I say *our* own, for although I am destined to depart this world alone, I am nonetheless intimately connected to my mother. From before the day I was born, the tuning of my identity has been exercised by my mother and her ways, for better or worse. The moment I was born, she caught me with not only a receiving blanket, but her own skin, and I've been getting caught up in it ever since.

My mother's womb is where the focusing of my story originates. Her wet, inner world my planet of origin, where the clay and soil she had gathered just for me became swept up in my story as I rushed through an opening inside of her.

My body is the silt and grit washed downstream and out from her own river, downstream from the many openings that came before mine. Downstream from my long ancestral river mother. One mother, one woman, one daughter, one girl with the heart of a river.

Some of the silt and grit that seed my form also comes from my father.

The pieces of my dad that break off of him at the places where the movement of storywater rubs against the edge of his awareness can get lodged into my own flow, encouraging it to shape and match his.

For example, when my father found out that he was having yet another girl, he purportedly shouted, "Fuck sticks!"

My mother found his boyish expression of superstition amusing and thought my identity needed to be stamped right in the middle with it.

What charming reactivity, father. My schoolyard nickname, no matter what state nor grade, I am always dubbed, "Winnow Stinks."

I suppose I can't entirely blame you, for even now in my eighth summer, I wet the bed nearly every night.

Winnow Stinks is a direct play on my name, but my other nickname, the one my sister and cousins call me, is more personal and to the point. They just call me "pee-pee."

My father thinks that a man who produces more female children than male has a "rotten sack."

I sometimes wonder where he got this particular magical river pebble from. Who shaped it and showed him how to use it? How long has it been clanking around in his head, bruising his thoughts, narrowing his story flow? How did it affect him as a young man and his developing view on the nature of men and women? Did he accept it easily, or did he give in to using it after a struggle?

I think about my gramma; a graceful, strong, intelligent woman, whose presence so vivid and real she must've had a balancing effect on the superstitious male magic he had to have been exposed to.

Gramma says superstitions are like cookie cutters that shape the storywater as it flows from the mystery into life. They are like magical objects that when jammed into the story faucet, they can block your mind from seeing anything else but the pattern they produce.

Gramma says you can feel powerful when you learn how to use them, but that you can forget how to appreciate or even remember what things are like before the shape is cut. She says they can trick you into believing that the shapes they make are permanent, reliable, and true. This makes them dangerous and destructive, if you believe that these things are you; if you give them your power and defend ideas over reality, and act out harmfully towards others who do not gather the water in the same way. Gramma says, this is why it is so important for moms and dads to sacrifice whatever ideas they can, so as to widen the flow in their children, because the wider the flow that runs through the people, the closer the universe comes to feeling whole.

Despite my father's influence, I like being a girl. For now. For now I am eight, and I am eavesdropping on my mother and her friend talking about sex, and something called an "orgasm."

Their feminine voices and excitement make me feel that there are secret things about being a girl that are waiting for me in the black box of time that I have to look forward to. I squint my eyes, trying desperately to peek into it, but I know I'm going to need some light to shine from the outside to figure this mystery out.

"What's an orgasm?" I ask, bounding from my hiding spot around the hallway and into the kitchen where my mother and her friend are talking.

The women look at each other before cracking up with laughter.

"The greatest feeling in the world," my mother's friend says, after a moment.

My mom scrunches up her brow, 'Shh," she says, jabbing her friend with stifled laughter and a slight elbow to the belly.

"Winnow, go to your room, I want to talk to your Aunt Crystal."

That's what my mom calls her friend, "Aunt Crystal."

Moments later, I lay on the floor of my bedroom. The thick, brown and gold mottled carpet enlivening my skin with the sensation of its scratchy-softness.

Mom tells me not to lay on the floor. She says floors are dirty. But I'd rather lay on a dirty floor than sit in a clean chair for a day, if given the choice. There's something about the way my blood flows calmly, evenly through my body that I love. When everything is quiet, I can hear and feel my blood pounding in every part of me, telling me our stories. Sometimes, the story is scary because there are deep emotions that run with it. Most of the time, the story is of many, many people. I can hear their heavy footsteps pounding up and down hills, in a never ending journey as far as I can see, in a long line. And the emotions. They run through every person on that long line. Sometimes I have to make myself get up when I can't bare to feel one more drop of the sadness they carry to me. But they carry joy, too. And courage.

I twirl the carpet with my fingers.

I make "carpet angels" with my arms and legs, then lie with my hands flat, letting the carpet erect between my fingers. I close them onto it, giving the carpet a pretend haircut.

The morning sun is coming through the window, closing my eyes and warming my skin. I am filled with the awareness of my body. My girl body.

Until recently, I have enjoyed shirtless summer days, played out under the sun, beneath trees and tall prairie grass, our skins touching, each habitual in form, complimentary to the other. But lately, mom has been telling me that my form will be changing and I'm not sure what I will end up as exactly, but whatever it is, it's not supposed to be out in the open anymore.

Will my form no longer compliment my environment?

I dunno, but mom says I have to wear shirts outside from now on. I'm supposed to get used to covering up the change that's coming. I wonder how I will be able to know it fully, if it's all covered up.

I can feel a fondness towards my developing femininity. I touch my skin, caring about how I feel.

I say to myself, "The greatest feeling in the world," as I bring my attention to the parts of me designated more girl than others.

I know those words have something to do with sex.

I take the time to remember one of my earliest memories.

I accompanied my parents to their friends' house, a married couple with two boys and one girl about me and my sister's ages.

When we arrived, the house was dark and the parents were watching a movie in the living room.

I took my coat off half way and stopped, transfixed by the sounds the people in the movie were making. They were new sounds, at least to my budding memory.

A woman and a man emerged from a small lagoon, naked, to the beach where they began to moan, the woman bending over in front of the man.

I stood there. The sound, the image, the emotion, all flowering into my awareness. Until my mom's friend noticed my blatant fascination, and quickly shushed me and my friends to go play.

We would visit these friends often in the summertime, and less during the school year.

In the summertime, we'd decorate areas under extensive thickets of brush with household objects.

In the late summer, the hazelnuts on those bushes would get big and green in their fuzzy coats. We'd pick them and put them in a pile. Not long after, big, fat grubs would start to come out of them, angry, perhaps, that we had placed their homes in a sunny, hot pile.

We'd throw the furry nut pods at each other, joyfully shrieking when a grub would land in our hair or fall down our shirts.

Our play would quickly escalate to picking up the grubs themselves and seeing how many ways we could terrify each other with them.

We never had the courage to eat any of them, but my sister touched one with her tongue once. She was proud of that, and I was proud of her, too.

When we weren't trying to gross each other out, our favorite thing to play in that underbrush was "house."

But the day of the dark house and naked people on the beach movie, we played a new game.

I don't remember who started it, but soon after closing the door between the world of adults and our world, the world of children, we had stripped off all our clothes and were reenacting the scene on the beach.

At the time, we didn't understand that we were mimicking a thing called "sex," or that the goal of sex is to put one thing into another, and we didn't distinguish sexual roles of man and woman.

A year later, when I was 6, we watched a video in school about what to do if someone touches you in the wrong places. When I was 4, mom asked me if anyone had ever touched me there, and told me to tell her if anyone ever did. Since then, mom's acted like the concepts of good and evil can be found originating from my feminine folds.

During the movie, I remember one of the little boys in my class whispering to the boy next to him, "I think they're going to fuck," after a part where an old man put his hands on the shoulders of a young girl.

I went home that day and asked my mom what "fuck" was. That got me a slap to the face and a bar of soap in my mouth.

I couldn't understand why my mother thought I should be punished for asking a question.

That's when asking questions first started to leave a bad taste in my mouth.

My mother couldn't hear them, but the questions started adding up.

I began to recognize them as being solely for me.

It was around this time that I started to understand that I couldn't get in trouble for what I was thinking. My thoughts became a safe place where everything inside of me could interact freely.

Sometimes I sit and think about things for hours, putting questions together in new ways, leading to more questions.

Occasionally, the things in my mind leave me feeling shameful. Like one time, not long after we watched that video in school, I was trying to understand the content of the video, and I imagined myself in the situation of the little girl. I questioned what would happen if one of my older male relatives were to play the role of the "toucher." I didn't really know any other adult males, so I used the faces I knew. To this day, I still don't know whether or not my 16 year old cousin actually told me, "I'll show you mine if you show me yours."

In my mind, keeping in toe with the video, I told on my cousin and he got sent away to a school for boys.

I was so ashamed I had thought up this scenario. I had the understanding that I could punish myself with my memories, so I told myself, "You'll never know if it was real or not."

And only two years later, my memory has developed in such a way that I really don't know if it was real, even though I remember telling myself that. I mean, I have a memory where I can see him standing on my gramma's picnic table outside, telling me this. It all seems real; the fantasy, the shame, and the curse of not knowing.

Whether or not I was daydreaming or dueling out punishments, I loved this space of mine.

This is when I began to part ways with my mother. I saw myself no longer of mostly her creation; I was becoming much more of my own.

"The greatest feeling in the world." I say to myself again and close my eyes, rubbing my girl parts harder, like a wish seeker with a magic lamp.

No, the beach scene didn't give me the greatest feeling in the world, but It did lead to further experimentation. I had wondered, "What do you do with this new kind of energy? What don't you do with it?"

On one of our visits to our friends' house, we paid close attention to our boy and girl parts when they were peeing.

I held the neighbor boy's thing while he peed.

He tried to hold my sister's.

We learned not to try that again, after some of the pee managed to land on the bathroom counter.

My sister's eyes lit up in amazement, and then panic. She quickly grabbed a little red cup and swept the pee from counter to cup before pouring it into the toilet.

This bit of happenstance led to the realization that we could pee right into the cup itself. I remember thinking, "Why doesn't everybody pee like this? Do people know they can do this? This is way funner!"

Our friends' older cousin, who was about ten, walked in and caught me squatting with the little red cup, and she slapped me hard on the back of the neck, spilling some pee on my socks.

"What are you doing?" she demanded.

I was furious at her until, "Drink it," she said, realizing what I was doing, her face turning from surprise to mischief. My madness fading to stupor.

After seeing the puzzled look on my face, she added, "Do it, or I'll tell your mom."

If you're guessing I did it, you're right. Don't be so surprised. I probably would have taken a sip at some point anyway, after remembering the intended function of cups. I would have done it in the name of investigation. And you know what? It's not the worst thing I have ever tasted. Dad's greasy mac soup with hamburger and onions? No thank you. Mom's stuffed peppers? I'd rather drink more pee.

My body calls for my attention.

My free hand digs into the carpet. I relax into the peak of a storm. Calm is brought forth from a center place. My center place. My girl epicenter. Shock waves of calm flood over me.

"The greatest feeling in the world," I think to myself, feeling like I had just discovered the secret hidden within the Great Pyramids of Egypt.

I wonder what I have after this to discover.

2

NINE

I DRAG MY fiNGER across the top of the shallow water, making ripples above a school of tiny fish. I pick up a stone and toss it at the far end of the school, plunging my hand into the water as they rush towards me. I pull my hand out, empty of little fish, as always.

My dad sits in the boxy, green Thunderbird with the windows down, "Walking on the Moon" by The Police fills the muggy summer air.

Little gnats dance around, and I imagine they are part of a great circus show, their movements choreographed by some unseen conductor of the whole of this summer's day. Every now and then, their dance troupe is thinned by a hungry, green dragonfly with metallic, kaleidoscope eyes; a kraken called forth from the sky seas for dramatic effect.

I follow the dragonfly and my curiosity for this stealthy predator along the river, and unlike my attempts at "fishing," my dragonfly-wrangling proves a success.

I close my fingertips upon its back as it sits digesting upon a clover. It brings its tail up in an arch to connect to my skin in a pinch. I fling it away in surprise and watch it resume its hunt.

I go up the embankment to the car where my dad sits, smoking with his friend Ted. The car's parked on a dusty old road, one of the many that run the reservation.

They're drinking beer. Alcohol is illegal on the reservation, but I don't know any adults who don't drink, besides gramma.

"Go play," he says, before I say anything.

I march back down the hill. I know what happens when you make dad angry. A drink of water isn't worth a butt whooping.

Butt whoopings are rare when we're out adventuring the reservation with dad, as there's not much tension between our behavior and dad's mood. There's so much open space, fresh air, and interesting animals to keep everyone happy.

I think Dad knows about the ways that nature acts as a self-disciplining force. He offers us up to the wilderness, and we are shaped by its green hand of discipline.

Things bite you if you don't respect them. You can freeze to death if you don't apply care to your well-being, same as you can get heat stroke from the sun. You recognize and appreciate the gift of fresh, clean water your body needs after spending time actively engaged in the elements of nature. If you are paying attention while immersed in this system, you will learn how to care for yourself and others. You will understand how important a sense of well-being is. And how easily it can be found when you are shaped in the discipline nature requires for survival.

"Winnow, look!" Maggie shouts to me, holding up a giant-sized frog. "Bet you can't beat this one!"

"Oh yeah? Bet I can!" I'm always up for a critter-catching contest.

We squish around in the mud, tall grass and cattails for about an hour before it starts to get dark and dad calls us to get going home.

"Hurry up now, the mosquitoes are coming out," Dad says.

But it was too late. By the time we all made it into the car, there were a good dozen of them trying to feast on my bare legs alone.

"Drive fast, Dad!" Maggie says.

Dad does. We all roll our windows down, and the mosquitoes get sucked out into the warm, summer air. Our enjoyment of the day is drawn out the window, trailing behind, tethering us to a shared wind of release. The day we inhaled, and in the evening we let it go, satisfied. We sleep in the dark, with bellies full of wilderness.

Dad is a hard worker. He's gone a lot of the time, and mom's most used tactic for getting Maggie and I to behave is to threaten us with the wrath of our father when he gets home.

I feel bad for my dad. Sometimes it's a couple of days between us doing something to get mom upset and dad coming home.

The bad thing about that is, our short term memory doesn't last that long. Within a few hours of mom promising a whooping from dad, we've already forgotten what we were in trouble for in the first place.

Our family routine has come to be so that whenever dad gets home, I just expect a butt whooping and fear seeing my father until said whoopings are handed out accordingly.

Sometimes as a prerequisite to a spanking, we get a smut on the forehead. I hate smuts. Unlike a spanking, you can see a smut coming. Everything moves in slow motion, and you have time to fear what's coming. And dad's fingers are big and strong.

I say I feel sorry for my dad, because who wants to be the face of fear in their children's eyes?

After a butt whooping, I usually just lay in my bed, and cry and think, "My daddy doesn't love me. Why does he hurt me?"

When dad's been home been for a while, and our crying has stopped, we emerge from our rooms eager to please him.

As you can imagine, there's a big difference between "house dad" and "adventure dad." I wonder what the differences in "house husband" and "adventure husband" are for mom. And what about for dad himself? Is there a "house Calvin" and an "adventure Calvin?"

It's Saturday afternoon. Dad's been gone working all week.

Dad's coming home in fifteen minutes. Better clean up your toys.

I stop what I'm doing. I look around. No one else is in the house. I close my eyes and feel what I had just been told. It hadn't really been in words. It was like how you feel after you read a sentence in a book and think about it and what it means. It felt like a cloud of thoughtful meaning had just passed through me. Or me through it.

"Don't pretend to know things," was what gramma had said to me the time I had come inside telling tall tales about fantastical creatures in the woods. I knew they weren't real, but at the time, at age five, I wanted to know what happened when you told adults about the things you make up in your head.

"It can be dangerous. You either know things or you don't. Sometimes, you will *kind* of know things, but you have to wait and get more information, more *story* to know them for sure."

I do an internal check. Had I thought this up? No. I had been counting my breaths for a long time, trying to reach 1000, when I came to possibly knowing this thing about dad being home soon. I decide I need more information, and leave the house in search for mom.

I find mom outside in the garden, transplanting jalapeño pepper seedlings. The soil here in Clearbrook, Minnesota where we live for the summer is rich and black. I love the way soil smells, whether it is full of clay and sand or the humus that fills the farmland, my body wants to acquire the essence. I know you're not supposed to eat dirt, but occasionally I will nibble on the flat clay rocks that melt in your mouth when you chew them.

"Mom, is dad coming home this weekend?"

It wasn't unusual for dad to be gone for weeks at a time.

"I'm not sure, Winnow. When he called on Thursday he said he might be home, but you know how your father's work schedule is."

"Well," I say, "I think he'll be home in 15 minutes."

Mom looks up from under her sunhat with an amused look on her face, like I had said something typically silly for a kid to say, "Fifteen minutes, huh?" She smiles at me. "Alright," she says, "well, I hope so."

This thing I knew was still bugging me. I couldn't know for sure if I really knew it unless I waited and made sure dad either did or did not come home.

I walk back into the house and sit down in the middle of the living room, and stare at the clock on the wall, the only one in the house. It has birds on it for each hour. Half past the bluebird. I know that means 1:30pm.

"Okay," I say, "if my brain didn't just make this thing up, dad should be home in about... ten minutes."

Ten minutes is a long time for a nine year old to just stare at a clock. Before I knew it, I was laying down, daydreaming about the life of the birds on that clock. Some were friends, others were secretive and didn't like it when the hands of the clock got near their imaginary nests.

"What the hell happened in here?" Dad's voice booms through my daydream.

I am at first in terror. I look around. I had forgotten the other part of my 'knowing': *better pick up your toys.* Shoot!

"You better pick up those toys, Winnow," dad says in a mean tone before adding, "but first come and give me a hug."

A big smile spreads across my face. "I knew you were going to be home soon. In fifteen minutes!" I tell him, hugging him as he bends over for the embrace, his stubbly chin scratching my cheek.

"I heard," he says, "your mom told me." He stands up and starts to chuckle, "Boy, you sure have her puzzled." Dad sounds amused, "You know what I think? I think you just missed your daddy," he says, patting me on the head. "Now go pick up your toys."

I skip over happily to pick up my toys, an act I usually find to be a punishment and waste of precious play time.

How did I know that? I wonder. Gramma was right. You either know things or you don't. And I knew it. But how? What did I know it with? Did *it* find *me*? Did it *know* me?

This knowing had me puzzled.

Mom let me call Gramma after dinner.

"Gramma, how do you know things if you don't know them with your eyes or with your nose or..."

Gramma giggles. I love the way Gramma giggles. It's like bubbles coming up from a mysterious, delicious soup that pop in your face to your delight, "Tell me what you know, my girl."

I tell Gramma the story and she sits quietly on the other side of the phone line. And then she says, "Winnow, I think you may have found your *in*. My advice would be, to take care of your *listening in*, and you will be surprised at what you will find listening back.

Listening in? Was this a *thing* that I have? Listening back? I ask her if that meant there were things other than me inside of me that were listening to me.

"There is more to us than meets the eye," Gramma says. "And the direction of inwardness fills the spaces between us all. And it's not really other *things* you will find when you look in, but yourself you will find, in other places, in other ways... in other ways of knowing."

"Like... finding my other bodies?" I ask.

"Yes, it's like that," Gramma says.

Gramma always seems to have a riddle for me.

"Oh," I say. Gramma knows that I will need to think on this.

"I love you my girl, I'll see you soon, gigawaabamin miinaawaa."

"Giga mii," I tell her and hang up the phone. It's what I've said to her since I was about three and couldn't say the whole phrase in Ojibwemowin. Now I just say it because it saves time.

It's Sunday morning and we are out for another summer drive with Dad. But today, we are going to the hardware store first before stopping at the boat landing down the road.

By the time I see it coming, it's too late.

"Ow!" I cover my forehead.

"What did I just tell you?" Dad's turned around from the driver's seat, voice low and rumbly. His hair is long, black, and un-gathered. His eyes are dark and deep, and his expression, I think, was maybe from as deep as hell itself.

I scan my memory. I have no idea what he had just told me. Part of me desperately grabs at the void, hoping to find something to satisfy him with.

"I said be quiet."

That made sense.

Maggie and I had been arguing about the middle, unused seat belt being too close to our legs, and were pushing it back and forth between us. Our argument had apparently escalated to smut-worthiness.

"If you don't be good in here, you're going to get a spanking. Do you understand me?"

Maggie and I nod our heads yes.

"Dad, can I sit in the car?" Maggie asks, looking at me, probably knowing the risk of a butt whooping was too high.

"If you stay in the car," Dad says.

"I will."

I follow Dad into the store. To me, the place looks like a maze of nuts and bolts. I don't know what anything in here is for. I assume this stuff is like toys for dads.

We came here because Dad is building a scaffold on the back of his pickup truck for hunting and fishing and he needs stuff to build it.

Dad's most happy when he gets to do "dad stuff" outside. Things like fishing, hunting, and harvesting wild rice are what keeps Dad "good busy."

He walks ahead of me towards a back room. When I look up, he has stopped and is talking to a guy in blue mechanic's clothes. He looks up and sees me getting curious about all the stuff in here. He drops his arm to his side, snaps his fingers and points at the floor next to him, maintaining an intense stare with me. I walk slowly to the spot, and wonder what Maggie's doing. I feel like I've walked into a den of boring, angry adults and there is no chance of getting back out into the fresh air where thoughts are as light as laughter.

I wonder if Dad tells himself he knows things about other people, about us kids. What does he think I'm going to do in here? Break everything? Steal? Don't pretend you know things, Dad, I tell him in my mind, looking up at him, hoping he will hear the words but not know they were coming from me. I'd die if he did. He'd probably kill me.

The guy brings Dad a little ways away to show him something. Phew. Finally I can move. He didn't tell me I could, but he also wasn't pointing me to stand anywhere in particular.

I notice a boy about my age in one of the isles. I walk over and see that he is picking his nose. He sticks his finger in his mouth. He notices me staring at him and he squints his eyes and balls his fist. He looks at me, then to a rack of baseball bats next to him. He punches one of the bats. The bats start falling off, making a loud, frightening sound. The sound of trouble. Our eyes widen. He must know what trouble is, too.

"I didn't do it!" I state loudly to my father, as I rush towards him.

"I didn't do it either," the little boy says, walking out of the isle slowly, bat in hand, tapping it on the bottom of a shelf.

"Andrius, get to the back and finish your lunch," the guy talking to my dad says.

Dad pinches me hard on the shoulder in disapproval.

"Go pick those up, then go to the car," Dad says.

I wipe a couple of tears from my eyes, and give a mean look to Andrius, who is smiling in the clear.

I smile too, when I realize I am free from the den of angry men.

After accompanying my dad to the boat landing, we drive home, which for the time being is a small farm house about five miles outside of the tiny town called Clearbrook, MN, and a half an hour drive from my gramma's house on the rez.

My mom is standing outside the house, her arms folded in front of her. She has been waiting for us.

"We have to get to Bemidji by five, my mom's plane will be coming in."

Mom is excited to see her mother, who she hasn't seen in years. My mom's mom, Gramma Ella, lives in California with my Grampa George.

"Mom, I'm hungry," I tell her as we are quickly ushered into the house to use the bathroom before the drive to Bemidji, the nearest "big" town of about 10,000 people and the closest with an airport.

"Grab an apple, Winnow, we don't have time for dinner until after your grandma gets here," Mom says, hands on my shoulders, steering me towards the toilet.

Mom is a woman of force, I think. She boasts often of her Celtic heritage and how she would rather fight someone than argue with them. Mom doesn't like to battle with wits or words. Mom's too feisty and impatient for that.

Despite Mom's temper, she always says that we shouldn't use the word "hate" when we talk about things, and that having hatred inside of us is a bad thing. Mom sure does hate lots of things though. She'd never say that what she feels inside of her is hate, but I know what hate looks like. Things Mom hates she just considers to be wrong. This is wrong, or that's wrong, and when things are wrong, Mom wells up with righteous 'right' feelings to counteract and correct the wrong ones. Usually with a pop to the nose or a declaration about the wrongness of the thing she can't physically fight.

We pick my Gramma Ella up from the airport. She looks just like how I remember her: short brown hair, brown eyes, tan skin, and she has an accent that I haven't heard since we went to visit her and Grampa in California when I was five. We also got to visit Dad's dad and brothers while we were there, his dad having developed an even more interesting accent; he sounded like a rezzy surfer.

Mom makes a dinner of pork chops with applesauce, mashed potatoes and peas. All foods I love. I wonder if she made the good stuff tonight not wanting a fuss from Maggie and me.

At about 8 p.m., Dad's left for work again and it's just us girls. It had started raining an hour before dinner and the sky was now booming and breaking with flashing bright.

"Hey guys, check this out," Maggie says from behind the front window curtains.

"Maggie, don't stand by the window, you could get struck by lightning," Mom says, pulling the curtain off of her and to the side.

"But Mom, look at the cows," Maggie says, pointing out across the field to the left, where the cows had lined themselves up in a straight row, every cow head steady and staring towards the back of our house.

Our nearest neighbor is at least a half mile away; there's nothing behind our house but a forest and dirt trail.

There is silence and stares, until we are startled by the thunderous sound of every cow in a break-neck stampede to move away from our house and whatever it was they were watching.

My Grandma Ella quickly walks out the front door and makes it nearly around the corner of the house, when my mom grabs her by the wrist, "Mom, get back in the house, it could be a bear." Grandma concedes and follows my mom back inside.

Our two dogs, Brutus and Biff, start barking in a dash around the house. We listen to them and their barks escalate into wild, crazed noises we'd never heard before. It's a sound that makes the hair stand up on my arms.

Before long, we can tell that the dogs are barking from inside of the little metal shed that is attached to the back of our house. Thing is, there isn't a way for them to get in there; the door is always locked. They must have *dug* themselves under the wall to get in.

After about twenty minutes, the panicked frenzy returns to normal dog barking sounds. The leaves on the trees quiet down as the rain lets up a little just in time for bed.

My room is the one with a window facing the woods behind the house. The glass had been broken out and is now covered with a thin, cloudy sheet of plastic. I stand quietly in front of the window in my darkened room. I can't see outside, but I can feel something out there. I lie down and close my eyes. I imagine myself standing at the edge of the woods, first looking towards our house, towards my own window, feeling myself in my bedroom, before turning to the woods and running deep. I fall asleep in the storm, searching for the mystery of the woodlands.

The next morning, us four girls are outside in the sunshine and wet of the world left behind from the storm. We are on a mission to investigate the strange activity of last night.

"Mom, Mom!" I hear Maggie's voice call from the start of the path that winds from the back of our house and off through the thick woods.

We all go to where Maggie is crouching near something on the ground.

"What is it?" Maggie asks mom.

"What in the world," Mom says, stooped over. She crouches next to Maggie. "One, two, three," she says, outlining the top of the footprint with her fingers. "It's got three toes," Mom says, looking up at her own mother. I realize then that my mother was looking for parental response of her own. "What do you think these are?" Mom asks Grandma Ella.

"Bear?" Grandma suggests mildly. The print looked like a human footprint only with three toes, not much if any arch, and it seemed wide in comparison to the length.

Mom rushes to the house and comes back with a tape measure.

"They're... eight inches long and... five inches wide," she says. She looks up the path, "Ho! There's more!" she says, pointing.

We find three more prints, all eight inches long by five inches wide at the toes, of which they all had three.

"It's an awful big gait," Mom says, "they're spaced five feet apart. I suppose whatever it was could have been running." She looks again to her mother and says, "You don't think... big foot?"

3

TEN

"OOH, I LIKE THIS one!" I tell my aunt, my imagination enlivened by features that would appeal to any kid.

"Let's see what else there is first, Winnow," my aunt says, her face looking like she just smelled something stinky.

After my parents divorced the summer I was nine, grand, majestic icebergs inside of me melted. The illusion of my sound environment melted away, flooding my inner landscape, opening up a big, watery space where a solid environment used to be. We traveled the cold and icy terrain, following the beat of our hearts, which I always thought were in rhythm.

The ices melted, along with our tiny footprints atop them showing my family's migration towards home, wherever that was I guess we never knew for sure. Our journey became washed up. My parents said they needed time to themselves, time apart. Just like that, we were disbanded like wanton travelers.

I stifle a tear.

Why don't we belong together anymore?

My sister Maggie stayed in Red Lake with my grand-mother, and I was sent to live with my Aunt Shelly in the middle of nowhere, Arkansas.

I was used to living in the middle of nowhere, but until now, my idea of nowhere included lots of lakes, animals, and people I love; nowhere being full of adventure from the inside out.

The yards of the few houses I saw during the last hour of our drive down here looked like the tops of ancient mens' heads; pale grass folding over in small patches here and there in barren comb-overs. I imagined the old men, their giant faces under the soil, bickering over who gets the last bit of water from the rains that last came during who knows what century.

Where does love come from?

Where does it go?

What *is* love?

Lately I find myself craving to be held. Not necessarily a physical holding, but a hold that embraces the things on my inside, shaping them, soothing them for me to recognize the inside of me as being "alright". While my aunt does her best, I still long for this. It's like a scream inside of me that makes my flesh tingle until it goes numb. If I don't do anything about it, I do feel numb, sometimes for days. But sometimes I look inward to this feeling, and try to do my best to hug it and soothe it myself. It usually works. I feel better, stronger, more empowered. But I also feel more alone, as the feeling that "maybe someone" or "maybe mommy or maybe daddy" will be there to make me feel better turns into a definite naught. I don't want to admit that I'm alone. I want there to be someone there for me. Sometimes, I see people who look nice, and I take from within me a feeling of "care" and I put it onto them. But it's only something that *I* feel. They don't have to feel a thing. They don't even have to know I exist. But it makes me feel less alone and more cared for from outside forces. Sometimes I wonder if doing this thing that I do to feel better could hurt me, like trying to know things I don't really know. But I do it when I'm too sad to look inside of myself, so I can never tell if it is good or bad to do.

"O-o-o-k-a-a-a-y," I say in faux defeat.

We walk up the hill, following the man in coveralls. He has a cigar in his mouth that he chews on between descriptions, "This one here," he says when we've reached the trailer at the top of the hill, "is a little bit more, but it's got a newer interior." He spits a soggy bit of tobacco beside the black, wrought iron stairs at the front door, bits of the juice clinging to his chin.

A rafter of turkeys wanders the dry, hilly trailer park. They stop to peck at the little foliage growing from the rocky, sandy soil. Woods line one side of the park, and the dusty road that doesn't see traffic but once or twice every afternoon lines the other. I see the turkeys from a distance, and get excited.

My auntie and I spend the afternoon cleaning the trailer at the top of the hill. A woman comes over to say hello. She has three girls with her. Claudia is the woman's name.

She is a little older than my auntie, but not by much. She introduces herself and her girls as Robin, Sarrah, and Ginny. They are ages twelve, nine, and six.

"Well that's good, because Winnow here is ten," my aunt says, and my new neighbors' eyes light up.

"Ten and a half," I remind her.

"Ten and a half." She rolls her eyes and gives me a squeeze on the top of the head.

"Can she come play with us?" the middle girl, Sarrah, asks.

"I don't know, we got a lot to do tonight." My aunt looks at me, scrutinizing.

The mother, Claudia, brings her attention closer to my aunt, "Do you dye your hair?"

"Yeah," my aunt says, and starts to laugh, "about every six months."

"It's a nice color on you. I could never pull it off," Claudia says, tugging on her medium brown bangs.

"Well, I suppose you can go play for a little bit, Winnow," my aunt says to me, motioning Claudia to come into our house to sit down. I can hear her talking about her fiery red hair as I fly out of the kitchen door into the Arkansas sun.

The next morning, I ask my aunt if I can go play with the neighbor girls. Robin wants to show me the collection of animals the land lord has along the edge of the property.

"What did you dream about?" my aunt asks, as recalling our dreams every morning has become one of our traditions over the last year or so we've spent together.

I cringe a little, the dream is still fresh in my limbs.

"Was it that bad?" she asks.

I nod my head yes.

"Well talking about it helps, you know that.'

I did know that. But some things I don't like to admit exist inside of me. Things that, although I didn't create them, I find them there. Like they rode in on the skin, and there's nothing I can do to keep them out.

"We were all sitting around at a big house with white paint and a front porch with white wooden railings. It was summertime and the grass was green and the driveway smelled like dry dust.

Someone found a tiny puppy, and everyone was gathering around it in the yard, everyone was following a shared draw towards it and feelings that were like waves around it; sensitivity, affection, delight. These feelings were shared by everyone in my dream.

Then my dad, who was sitting on the porch next to me, I could see something pushing these feelings out of him. When he felt these feelings and saw that everyone else was feeling them too, he let something push the lightness out from inside of him. It was a blackness. And it grew until it filled a boundary as big as his body.

He became powerful when it grew so big inside of him that he actually thought *he* was *it*. I knew what he was going to do when he got up and walked out to the yard where the puppy was. He needed to draw attention to this thing inside of him; he wanted to show it to the people who were seeing only light.

He evoked the darkness that the effect the death of an animal has on those who have come to care about it, and he brought it to the beginning of the puppy's life, and to the skin of the people who had wrapped themselves up in only the colors of the lightness of life in that moment.

I cried out for him to stop, falling in weakness at the feet of his intention before I could rise to stop him. He took the puppy and raised it high into the air above the people's heads, making them look in a different direction, towards the dark movement of skin he had gathered and now held above their heads, before plummeting it to the ground, again and again. And Aunty, he was smiling."

My aunt sat quiet, motionless across from me at the breakfast table, "Jeez, Win."

"I don't think he was being evil, though. I could see the black that formed his body. It stretched out beyond his lifetime. I think he was shown that darkness when he was little. Maybe someone in his family killed one of his animals because they couldn't take care of it, I don't know.

But the darkness didn't seem wrong. It looked like any other of the flows of color that cross the skin. It only looked out of place in him. It was like the color had made such an impression on him that he was holding onto it. He didn't know how to let it go, and it just flooded him until he exploded in an overuse of the color.

He was showing everyone what was tormenting him on the inside by splashing that color all around the inside of everyone else. And when he saw the color all over everyone else, it made him feel like he had gotten rid of some of it that had been stuck inside him. And he felt better.

I don't think he was ever taught what to do with it. He was shown it, and then was left to deal with the darkness from inside the darkness." It made me sad to think of my father suffering like this, "I don't think he ever found his way out. It's like his body grew up, but his skin didn't. Or, he didn't let it. Some things are too painful to know how to let go of unless you're shown, I guess."

My auntie just sits there. I can almost see that color in her now, too. And I can see that she has wrapped herself up in sensitive skin, and so I don't bother to tell her about the other dreams I had.

She says I can go play, and to mind my manners if I go to the neighbor's house. I promise I will and loudly slurp cereal flavored milk from my bowl.

"Winnow," she says, disapproving.

I grin and put my bowl in the sink.

"What is that thing?" I ask Robin. She just turned twelve, but I think her breasts are large for . They're almost as big as my auntie's. I can't help but look up to her. She's quite lovely. She acts like a girl, but looks more like a woman.

"An echidna," Robin says, dropping a few ants into its open-top enclosure. The echidna's tongue sticks out the end of its long beak, licking up an ant. We giggle.

"His name is Puggle," Robin adds, "it means baby."

"But Bill says he's almost twenty years old," Robin's younger sister, Sarrah adds. "He also says it's got a four-headed penis!"

"Shut up, dufus," Robin tells her, putting her hands around Sarrah's neck, as if to choke her.

Sarrah pretends to pass out, and says with her eyes still closed, "I wish I had a four-headed penis," and bursts into wild laughter, running away as Robin chases after her towards their trailer.

It's nice having girls my age to talk to and push boundaries with.

I wonder how long it will be before Robin joins the cult of adulthood.

I've never lived in one place long enough to develop lasting friendships. The longest stretch I've lived in one place at a time was ten months, eleven days. Just long enough to start and finish the third grade in Red Lake.

I've lived on and off the reservation growing up, but now that my parents are divorced and my auntie and myself have moved away, I'm not sure when I'll be back. Or when my parents will, either. My mom isn't from the reservation. And me and my sister were never enrolled.

I like these girls. I wonder how long we'll stay here in Arkansas. I follow behind them, trying to catch up.

There is an accent that a lot of Red Lakers have. I have it a little bit. I wonder how long it'll take, living off of the rez, to get an Arkansas accent.

My auntie's already practicing hers. She thinks saying "ya'll" and "yaunt to" is funny, and has been throwing it into conversations whenever possible. She thinks it's cute, but it makes me feel like she's trying too hard to forget where we came from.

"But auntie, Sarrah is too much of a kid for me," I say in protest.

"Winnow, Claudia says Sarrah likes you and asked if she can stay the night. Sarrah's nine and your ten. That's not much of a difference. Don't yaunt to make friends with her?"

I just stare at her. I can see the smile creeping up the side of her mouth, but I ignore it. This is serious stuff.

My aunt's adult logic is sound, but it is no match for the will of a preteen, "But auntie, I'm closer to Robin. She *just* turned twelve. I'm *almost* eleven. And Sarrah *just* turned nine. She's closer to eight and I'm closer to twelve," I can feel my emotions rising up inside of me, heated by the fire of change and wanting to be more than what I am.

"I see your point," Auntie says.

I relax a little, feeling a bit understood. That's all I wanted.

"You can be friends with both Robin *and* Sarrah, you know, if yaunt to." She gives me a sideways glance, and seeing that I'm not quite ready for jokes adds, "You can have friends that are kids and friends that are almost teens. That's just where you're at right now. Half-way to being an adult. There's nothing wrong with having more than one kind of friend." She looks at me with her "kind eyes," and picks up the phone, "Call her. Dinner will be ready in about an hour. Ask her if she likes spaghetti."

I was really only protesting against hanging out with Sarrah because earlier that week, one of Robin's friends, who is also twelve, came to our trailer park to visit Robin and spend the night. They whispered secrets to each other, and when we were playing "makeover" just earlier, they thought it was funny to try and curl my hair in a way that made me look more childish. I was not amused.

I sigh, feeling a wave of relief wash over me. Maybe it was okay to have both kinds of friends.

I grab the phone from my aunt, who had already dialed their number after seeing the expression on my face change, "Hi Sarrah, my auntie says you can come over and spend the night. Do you like spaghetti?"

About an hour later, we put our dishes away, mine still holding chunks of hamburger pushed far to the edge of my plate.

"Winnow, finish your supper before you go play." Auntie knows I hate hamburger meat.

"But auntie, I ate *some* of it," I say in protest. My stomach weakens at the thought of having to eat another bite.

"Sarrah ate all of hers," Auntie says, as if I could be jealous of a hamburger eater.

"I love hamburger," Sarrah says, licking her plate clean.

I wince at the sight of her face, covered in sauce.

"How about if I do the dishes instead?" I venture.

"How about you do the dishes anyway?" my aunt says, smartly.

I fold in defeat, and shovel the large spoonful of meat into my mouth and under my tongue. I make an awful face and pretend to chew and swallow. My aunt doesn't say anything, just pats my head, takes my plate from me and turns to the sink.

She bought it.

I walk down the hall as calmly as I can and spit the hamburger into the toilet. I pee too, just in case she's listening.

Sarrah comes into the bathroom when I'm still on the toilet with my pants down.

"Hey! Get out of here!" I yell at her, pointing towards the door.

"Shh!" she says and peeks out the door, looking for my aunt.

She giggles and says, "I have sisters, you know. It's no big deal."

She's standing with her hands on her hips, swaying from side to side, and says, "Let's see it."

Not planning on sitting on the toilet all night, and also not wanting to get her in trouble, I consider her position. I know what it's like to share everything with a sister. I summon the courage to open up my private world for her to look into, and I stand, pulling up my panties.

"Nice underwear," she says, lifting her brow up and down in emphasis, a huge smile on her reddening face.

"Shut up," I tell her, before pulling them up high enough to give myself a wedgie, "how's this?" I ask.

"Let me see the back," she says, cocking her head to one side.

I do a twirl, and she pokes me in the butt cheek. I slap her hand away and pull my pants up.

"Yup, looks good," she says.

"Wash your face," I tell her, not knowing what else to say.

She looks at herself in the mirror, then turns to me and leans forward, cheeks orangish-red with sauce, lips puckered, "How about a kiss?" she says.

"Don't be silly," I say, frowning at her.

She just stares at me. I realize that her silliness was an extension of her seriousness. She's looking at me; vulnerable, rejected. I realize that she actually wants to kiss me.

I hadn't done any sort of experimenting with other kids since I was eight, and I was proud of that. I knew that playing naked must be a normal thing for kids to do, and I also knew that it had to stop at some point. I had made up my mind that eight was the cut off for me, personally.

And I was happy with that decision. I was growing up. But this felt different.

The stuff when I was younger was no doubt play. I didn't do the things I did because I was *attracted* to my neighborhood friends. Attraction was something that I had felt a handful of times back then, but it had never been plugged into my childhood experimentation. That connection was never made.

Until this point, I had only been attracted to boys, even though I had experimented with our friend that was a girl. I hadn't made any distinction between female and male sexuality.

And I probably wouldn't have thought about kissing her, had she said nothing.

I add, "I'm not going to kiss you with sauce all over your face."

Her eyes grow wide, as does her smile. She turns to the sink and quickly scrubs away the drying bits of tomato and Parmesan cheese.

She pats her face dry on a hand towel.

She turns to me, gently, with the smallest, shyest smile I'd ever seen, and brings her face to mine. I can feel the softness of her skin, melting away the hardness of mine.

My heart races, moving my blood fast, sending tingles through my body.

"You're sexy," she says, and kisses me gently.

She cups my face in her hands, and pushes me into the wall with her body. I can't help but wonder if she is still in her childish experimenting phase, but there is something present between us that tells me she is not. I let go of thought, and allow myself to just feel.

Sarrah sleeps next to me in my twin-sized bed. We're in our pajamas, and she's hugging me in her sleep.

I smile to myself. I never thought that my first real kiss would be with a girl.

School in Arkansas is a lot different than school in Red Lake, but not much different from schools elsewhere.

Lunch time has always been stressful for me.

On the reservation, everyone gets to eat. You just stand in line and you get food.

Off of the reservation, schools require either money, or some form of lunch tickets.

There are three types of lunch tickets here: full price, reduced price, and free lunch. My aunt says I'm supposed to get free lunch.

But my aunt says this to *me*. At our *house*.

She doesn't realize that simply telling me I get free lunch doesn't mean I actually get to eat at school. There's paperwork you have to fill out for that. My aunt hates paperwork. Any time she has to fill anything out in print, she oozes anxiety.

I pretty much gave up trying to explain to her how hungry I'd get by the end of the day. I'd cry about it sometimes, and wonder if it meant she didn't love me as much as she said she did.

Half of the time we have cereal to eat at home before I spend an hour on the bus just to get to school. Most schools I've been to have free breakfast if you get there early enough, which I usually don't. When I do, it feels like life is a little bit sweeter. I feel like I can relax, even though I'm not sure what lunch time will bring, besides anxiety.

There is a validation associated with this anxiety, or more like a lack of validation, as I feel like I am not a valid part of society. If I don't even get to eat, how could I possibly feel like part of this overwhelmingly large thing I try so hard to understand and fit into?

Remember how I said that I'd sometimes take my own feeling of "care" from inside of myself and put it onto other people? Well, that feeling of "care" now has the feeling of being validated attached to it. It's like I'm constantly looking for someone else to tell me I'm alright, that they care about me, and that I'm part of something whole. I feel desperate.

Anyway, when I don't make it to breakfast on time at school, I get sad, and spend the morning pretending I don't *need* to eat. By the time lunch time comes around, I snub it like it's an old enemy I'm too cool for.

It's gotten to be so that when I go to other people's houses after school, I act like I'm not hungry. It reduces the chance that I'll feel let down. It makes me feel more in control of the situation.

"When I was in school, we'd all just get free lunch. Winnow, tell them you get free lunch," my aunt would say, conjuring up memories of when she was in school to complete her investigation into the matter. And I could hear the frustration in her voice if I tried to push the subject beyond her investigation, like I was cornering her into feeling the way she did.

So, for the last year, I haven't been eating regularly at school.

Once or twice a month, my teacher gives me two or three tickets that she pulls from her purse. They look different from student tickets, so I think they must be the kind that teachers get to eat with.

One of the lunch ladies gave me a suspicious look when I handed her the blue ticket for the first time instead of a red one, like she thought maybe I had stolen it. My teacher, who happened to be right behind me in the lunch line that day, told her it was alright, and I haven't had a problem with it since.

Sometimes I'm too hungry to concentrate at school. And when I get home, I'm agitated and feel like I want to shut everyone out. Like everyone else is to blame for how I feel and I hate them for it.

Today is one of those days. I missed breakfast *and* lunch. I didn't bother going home after school before coming down here to the little creek that runs not far from the bus stop. I'd rather get in trouble and be sent to my room. I don't want to look at my aunt's face today, anyway. She'll probably set me off on some unimportant chore as punishment when I get home, oblivious to my problems. I came down here because I wanted to get in some space for myself. And Sarrah. I'm learning to let her into my world when I feel like this.

I let my flip flops slide off of my feet and onto the warm rocks below the low, wooden bridge I'm sitting on. The rocks are usually scorching hot from the high sun, but today the sky is cloudy, like my insides.

I dunk my feet into the warm water. My pinky toe is broken again, but it doesn't hurt in a bad way.

When I was four, I was doing somersaults on the wooden floor of my dad's friend's house. I remember feeling an intense, new feeling but I couldn't tell where it was coming from. I took time to inspect my arms and legs. When I got to my feet, I saw a white circle stuck on the bottom of my foot. I touched it, and the sensation flooded my senses. I pulled on it and it revealed itself to be a thumbtack. As soon as I had pulled it out, the new feeling stopped, and I felt sadness about the shortness of the experience. I replaced the tack in its hole and sat hugging my foot into my body, doing my best to appreciate the new thing I knew I'd soon loose, and wondered when and where I'd encounter it again.

I've learned that the novelty of pain wears off quick, but its presence can become reliable and familiar.

Crawdads scurry on the bottom of the creek, looking for drowned bugs or whatever they can find to eat. I almost envy those crawdads in their free world of effort and reward. I bet even they get to eat more than I do, I think.

I'm waiting for Sarrah to show up. We come here everyday after school, but I have to wait for her even though I take the bus and she gets a ride from her mom, because they have to stop at three different schools. Arkansas is weird like that. Or, at least this school district is. There's like six different schools separating grades before you even get to high school. I'm not in school with Robin *or* Sarrah.

I wish she'd hurry up.

I feel like I could cry. I want to tell her how I hate feeling like a neglected animal.

I feel like a homeless rez dog.

Rez dogs don't seek out affection much, if ever. But they are constantly in search of food. They follow people around, hoping to land a scrap here and there.

That's what I felt like today.

I'm a loner at school. Sometimes I hang out with this other loner girl who people make fun of for whatever stupid reason they decide on that day.

Today, I sat with her at lunch, listening to her talk. I couldn't stop fidgeting. I had to stop myself from staring at her food. It takes willpower to act uninterested in something very basic like food when you're hungry.

When she was finished eating, she had an almost full bag of fruit snacks that she didn't want. She put it in her now empty-but-for-crumbs plastic sandwich bag and squeezed them tight in her fist. Just before cramming them into her used paper lunch bag, she looked at me, then opened her fist and said, "You can have these if you want."

It's hard to describe the way I felt in that moment.

I felt desperate. I felt ashamed. I felt angry.

But mostly, I felt relief from all these things.

"Sure... I'll have'em," I said, as casually as I could. One girl's garbage is another's afternoon salvation, right?

Sarrah skips over to me, her short, brown, wavy hair bouncing merrily.

I listen to her talk for a bit. She's super excited, and it's hard for me to follow along.

But then she says something that I do understand, "So Mary Beth got mad at me because I kept biting her tongue..."

"What?" I said, my first contribution to the conversation. I can feel jealous heat building up inside of me. I've never felt like this before.

I've heard adults talk about people cheating on each other, but had never bothered to try and understand what it would be like to cheat or be cheated on. I've never been part of a couple.

I realize that I want her to only be with me.

I don't understand my feelings of jealousy. This is a whole new circumstance birthing this already known feeling that has until thus far, shown up in situations outside of the arena of sexual attraction.

I tell her, "I don't want to kiss you if you're kissing other girls."

Then something happens to her face. The giddiness drains from it. She starts to look upset, worried, then almost panicked.

"Do you kiss boys, too?" I ask, from this new place of vulnerability and entanglement.

"I don't like boys," she says.

She sits down beside me, and puts her arm around my shoulder.

I stiffen, and look away from her. She tries to pull my face towards hers, but I resist, and repeat, "I mean it, I don't want to be your girlfriend if you're kissing other girls."

It was the first time I had used the word "girlfriend" in a sentence that involved myself. In reality. And I never imagined I could use it to describe myself and and another girl. That's just not the way people talk around here, or anywhere I've been.

"I won't!" she says quickly, "I promise, I'll stop!"

I feel relieved. I believe her. It's not like we had talked about any of this. It's not like the idea had occurred to either of us. Exclusivity. Investment of our feelings in the other person, alone. We could make something just for us.

"Please look at me," Sarrah says, sadly.

I look at her. Our eyes meet at the birth of a new place. She grabs my hand, and tucks it between her knees, and reaches out, pulling me closer to her.

We nestle for a minute or so, both a little teary eyed. I tell her about what happened today, and she listens, but doesn't seem to fully understand how I feel.

"Why don't you eat lunch?" she says, like she's never heard of such a thing. "Do you want to come over to my house for supper?"

"I'll have to ask my aunt, but I don't know if she'll let me. I didn't go home when I got off of the bus."

"Do you think she'd let you spend the night? Robin's at Lilah's house," she says.

"Maybe, if I'm really nice to her for a couple of hours before dinner," I smile at the possibility of weaseling my way out of my aunt's reach by buttering her up with the exaggerated affection she loves so that I could practice a more subtle affection with Sarrah.

She stands up and grabs my hand, and we climb down the rocks to the creek. We splash around a while, softening the edges of our emotions, before walking home, holding hands.

My aunt decided to let me spend the night at Sarrah's house, as she had a date. She practically pushed me out the door.

I walk over to Sarrah, who is bouncing up and down on her porch with glee. I look around nervously to see if anyone is listening, before I tell her, "I have something my aunt gave me."

"What is it?" she asks, trying to dig into my backpack, but I turn out of her reach.

"Not here!" I laugh.

We hurry to her bedroom, I wave hello to her mother on the way.

Sarrah closes the bedroom door behind us and asks, "What is it?"

I plop down onto the bottom bunk bed, and dig into my bag. I pull out a porno magazine. Sarrah's eyes widen, and she giggles.

"Oh my god!" she says, grabbing it out of my hands, "your aunt gave this to you?"

"Yeah, I told her that my health teacher was talking about sexually transmitted diseases, but he didn't say how you get them. My aunt didn't know how else to describe what sex and male and female organs do and what they look like, so she gave me this. She must keep them stashed somewhere."

We bust out in laughter at the thought of my aunt sitting around looking at pornography.

"My parents have videos," Sarrah says.

I get excited. I've never seen a porno before.

She walks to her desk and digs underneath a narrow spot between the bottom drawer and the floor. She pulls out a VHS tape.

"She thinks my dad took it with him," she says. Her dad is frequently out of town on business.

"My mom's going to the store," she says, grinning at me, dancing the tape around in front of my face.

A little while later, we are in her mother's bedroom. Sarrah sticks the tape into a VHS player that is attached to a small, black and white television.

I sit on her mom's bed. She grabs the remote, adjusting the volume so we can hear the tape, but also hear if her mom comes home.

There is a man in a red and white dress shirt. He says but one or two lines to a large breasted woman before telling her to take her clothes off. Sarrah fast forwards the tape about a minute, and says, "You have to see this."

She stops at a scene where two women are kissing. Sarrah puts the remote down, and leans toward the TV.

I just watch Sarrah. I hear the women moaning and the sound of lips smacking. I understand what she said about not liking boys. She really is only interested in girls.

A few minutes later, we hear the sound of her mother's car in the driveway. The store's only a few miles away.

She ejects the tape, shuts the television off quickly, and we run down the hallway to her bedroom at the other end of the house, laughing the whole way.

4
ELEVEN

SARRAH MOVED AWAY THIS past winter. She was a lot more upset than I was. We both felt helpless in the situation, but I was already familiar with how it felt to lose people I cared about. Sarrah wasn't.

The day they left, her sister Robin teased her, saying, "Kiss your girlfriend goodbye," and called her "gay girl".

Sarrah got super mad and fought with her sister. She looked like the Tasmanian devil from the cartoons, chasing her sister all over the trailer court, swinging her fists, her face red.

In a strange, upside-down way, it felt good to know that things like loss are reccurring. It made both the loss of Sarrah, and that of my family seem like they were one and the same thing. That loss isn't for just one person at one time, but really is an entity in its own right, that it is a whole, and we are each responsible for carrying our part of its wholeness. For allowing our part of its wholeness into our lives. For giving it a chance to live.

It was then that I began to develop a warming up to it, a friendship, you might call it. For unlike my family, the things that move on my inside are things I am learning I can count on to be there, if I don't try and push them out. Sarrah had helped me thread back into my life a feeling of self care; I haven't tried to push it out of me much since. It was for me. *I* have to care.

I haven't had anyone close to me since Sarrah.

Tribeless

I moved with my aunt to Bemidji, Minnesota after the school year was over. My aunt followed an old boyfriend, Billy. I followed my aunt.

I was glad to be so close to home. Red Lake is just a half hour drive from Bemidji, so I got to see my sister and grandmother about once a month on the reservation.

About a year before we moved back to Minnesota, my uncle Mitchell got sent to jail for beating up his girlfriend. He also set her car on fire. She bruised him up good too; she took a knocking stick used for harvesting wild rice to his skull and ribs.

He's out of jail now and has been in AA for three months. He's a lot different when he's sober; he's a pretty sad guy. He says he's always been sad, only the alcohol helped him forget it.

My uncle likes fishing, and has taken Maggie and me along a couple of times so far this summer. Today, he's taking us fishing west of Red Lake, and we've convinced him to drop us off at our favorite spot that has the remnants of an old stone building alongside a creek.

"Now don't drop that pole in the water," my uncle instructs my sister before heading to his own favorite spot about a mile further down the road.

Maggie's thirteen now. She loves to fish, hunt, and do everything she can independently outdoors. Today, she's going to teach me to fish. The other times I tagged along with her and my uncle, I spent the entire time playing in the water and trying to catch crawling things and avoiding the leeches.

After my uncle leaves, we play for a short time in the ruins. The old stone provides a cool contrast to the midday summer heat.

We see an unfamiliar little island near the bank of the creek and poke it with a stick to see if it's sturdy enough to step on.

"Eee!" we both squeal in surprise when a head pokes up out of the water. We laugh in delight when we realize it's a giant snapping turtle covered in water plants and algae.

I stare into its eyes before it submerges and moves upstream.

"Come on, Pee-Pee, let's get some fish," Maggie says.

"Shut up," I tell her. She knows I hate it when she calls me that. I haven't wet the bed since I was eight.

"I'm just kidding, jeez." She ruffles my hair, "Come on!" She picks up the fishing pole and we run across the road to the mouth of the creek where the water has less plants and the fish are easier to see.

"Whoa, check out that monster!" Maggie excitedly casts out and I sit down near the edge of the water.

"Don't move fast," she tells me.

"I know," I say.

"Boozhoo girls," a voice says from behind us.

We turn to see a man in a uniform.

"Boozhoo," Maggie says.

"Is that a cop?" I whisper to Maggie.

"No, it's DNR," she says.

"Oh, good," I say.

"Catch anything?" he asks Maggie.

"Not yet," she says.

"You girls from Red Lake?" he asks, looking at me.

"Yes," Maggie says.

"Are you enrolled?" He looks at Maggie.

"No, but my dad is. And we're from White Earth, too, but we're not enrolled there either," she says.

"Okay," he says, reaching his hand out, "give me the pole."

"What? Why? It's my uncle's pole! You can't take it," she says.

"If you're not a member and your dad isn't here, I have to take it," he says, opening and closing his fingers into his palm. "Give it here."

Maggie looks devastated. She hands him the fishing pole.

"You girls have a nice day now," he says smiling and walks back up to his truck parked on the side of the road.

"Can he do that?" I ask Maggie. "But we're from Red Lake."

"Guess we're not," Maggie says, tears in her eyes. "Uncle's going to kill me."

Our uncle was upset, but he had compassion for Maggie, and tried to make her feel better by calling the DNR agent a few choice words.

"You're a Red Laker," he says, "no one can tell you different just because you ain't got a piece of paper."

But even I knew that might not be true.

In an attempt to cheer her up he says, "You could always marry a Red Laker. What about Travis?" He elbows her playfully. Apparently Travis is a guy Maggie has a crush on.

She smiles, but I can tell she's still upset.

Maggie didn't want to do much outside by herself after that. She did however, start "chasing" boys, as aunt Shelly would say. But I knew what she was really chasing. If you ask me, Maggie started chasing what she was taught was her "Indian-ness" was.

5

TWELVE

MY AUNT'S BOYFRIEND BILLY turned out to be a two-timing cheater. Shortly after they broke up, we moved to Texas.

I don't know what my aunt saw in Billy. She said she was in love.

What people call "love" was starting to show itself to be an unstable, erratic, self-bloating, self-deflating, constructed thing. Love is something that hasn't shown itself to me yet in its natural flow, like loss has. But I get the sense that it must indeed be there, however lost or buried, or simply unfound. I was afraid to know what my aunt thought love was, so I never asked.

Is it love that comes to us?

Or is it us to it?

Are we creating new descriptions for love?

Do we create because we do not posses?

What *is* love?

I'm starting to think that the feeling of love and the act of love are two different things.

When I was a kid, my parents would tell us they loved us every night before bed, if they were home, that is.

They would tell us they loved us, even after a day of shouting, spanking, and my mom's borrowed line from popular culture, "I brought you into this world, and I can take you out".

My mom says she's anti-abortion. But apparently killing an eight year old over an unborn fetus makes more sense to her. I think she would tell me that because she didn't know what to say when she felt the way that she did. And even if it's really just a saying, why would you want that idea in your kid's head? I mean, why would you want to tell your child that you *can* take them out of the world, i.e., murder them, and that apparently this is an accepted behavior? A warranted one? Is your child's behavior so bad that you want to make them think that they're is death-worthy under your rule? How is that not a terroristic threat against someone you proclaim to love? What do you expect your kid to think of you if you paint that logic into their nurture-seeking mind?

Anyway, my aunt's current boyfriend is even worse than Billy.

We were at the grocery store. My aunt was getting snacks for work, and some guy started commenting on how bad the mini cakes she loves are for her.

I noticed an excitement in my aunt's eyes. Like she was looking at something she admired but didn't have. She looked at this guy like he had it. I could see her demeanor turn to self doubt. She started moving her arms fast, and nodding her head and saying yes to whatever he was saying.

Anyways, this guy must have told her he could get her in shape. I think he must like a project. My aunt hates exercise.

A couple of days later, I'm at the kitchen table, eating oatmeal on a Saturday morning.

I'm in my pajamas. I don't really have much in the way of boobs yet, but I've moved up to a size A from a AA.

I'm not wearing my training bra, and my nipples are noticeable through my white tank top.

My hair is messy. My hair's always messy. I've always had long, messy hair.

My mom used to get fed up with brushing my hair, because tangled into it, there'd always be sticks, dried food, and whatever else my day had thrown at my head. She'd throw her hands up in the air and wait till my dad got home and tell him to do it. My father, to try and make a week's worth of impact on my behavior, would brush it hard on purpose when it was full of knots. I would cry and he would tell me it was my fault. Then he'd send me to my room because he didn't want to hear to me cry. My heart would fill and then drain of feelings of love for him.

Anyway, this guy comes to the screen door in the kitchen. He's wearing short white shorts and a blue muscle shirt. He's bouncing from side to side at a slower and slower pace.

When he comes to a stop, he cups his hands around his face and looks in through the screen, "Well, hel-lo," he says, in a tone that makes me sink my chest down to hide my swollen nipples under the edge of the table.

"Hi," I say.

He opens the door and steps inside. I nearly fall out of my chair.

"Whoa, easy there!" he says, holding his hands up in front of his body, "I'm a friend of your aunt."

My belly does a few flip flops.

Oh, no.

I feel sick to my stomach. Not a new boyfriend. I was just getting used to spending time with my aunt again, and now this guy's going to be her new obsession. I recognize him then to be the mini cake hater from the store.

My aunt's not herself when she's obsessing over a guy. When it's just us, she's warm, patient, inquisitive, and she listens to me. Sometimes.

"My aunt isn't home from work yet," I tell him.

My aunt started working overnights as a CNA at the old folks home about ten minutes away.

"Okay, well, she'll be here soon, right? Do you mind if I wait?" he asks, pulling up a chair a foot or two next to mine.

"I don't care," I tell him, but I really just want to get away from him so that I can watch Saturday morning cartoons.

He holds out his hand for me to shake. I grab it and he smoothes his thumb over my hand, "I'm Jim," he says. I feel like my secret sexual feelings are being pried into and coaxed to come out of their spot where I keep them safe.

"How old are you, nineteen?" he grins at me.

"I'm twelve," I tell him, like it should be obvious.

"Looks like you really love your pillow," he says, reaching up to feel my hair. I freeze in my seat. "Sure doesn't look like it likes you, though."

"I'm not that much older than you, you know," he says, lowering his hand from my hair, placing it on his abdomen, where he lifts up his shirt just enough so I can see his stomach muscles and a small amount of pubic hair. I feel myself getting sexually aroused and nauseated at the same time.

We sit silently, until I give up and ask him what he wants to hear, "How old are you?"

"Twenty-six," he says.

I think that's old.

"I bet you have a lot of boyfriends," he says, winking at me.

"No. I don't even know anyone here yet," I say, sharing a bit of my vulnerability in regards to my new environment without thinking about it.

"Well, you know *me*," he says. "I just live a block over. My house is the red one with the white shed and the green Volkswagen..." he trailed off, waiting for some sign from me as to whether or not I knew which place was his.

I nod. I knew which one he meant.

"I have a trampoline. You're free to jump on it whenever you want."

I had seen the trampoline the day we moved in, and had wondered if there were kids that lived there that I could play with.

"Do you have kids?" I ask.

He laughs, "Nope. I don't have time for them."

I find his answer dishonest. I'm a kid, sort of, and he seems to have time for me. This guy's got "big phony" written all over his skin.

My aunt pulls up in the driveway. Jim gets up and walks outside. I quickly make my escape to the living room and turn on the Saturday morning cartoons at a quiet level, pulling my blanket up to my chin so that I can masturbate without being caught.

A few of weeks later, my aunt brings me to the pool. It's the middle of summer, in Texas. The pool is my new favorite place in the universe.

Believe it or not, with all the lakes in Minnesota, it was a pool in Texas where I learned how to swim.

My aunt got us summer passes after Jim insisted that pool time was just what she needed to round out her physical fitness routine. He had also paid the extra ten bucks so I could get the cute blue two-piece bathing suit I wanted, instead of the drab grey one-piece my aunt wanted to get me, the only one that kind of fit me on the discount rack.

Jim could suggest anything to her, and she'd jump at the chance to change herself for him.

When Jim told her she'd make a sexy blonde, the next morning after work she rushed right over to the salon and had it dyed, even though she had to sell some of our things to make up for the rent money a few days later.

When he suggested we attend services at the church he went to, that Sunday we were sitting in the front row.

I was really starting to hate Jim, until he suggested she buy us both summer pool passes. Then I tried my hardest to be grateful for the opportunity, even though it made me sad to think that my aunt would never do anything like that for the sake of our enjoyment without the prompting of a boyfriend.

Every day at the pool, I would push myself to go a little bit further into the deep end, learning what I was and was not capable of. I learned how to trust my body in the water, and felt good about challenging myself, letting go of my mental hurdles with determination.

It's a Wednesday, and my aunt and I just arrived at the pool. We put our clothes in the lockers and rinse off in our bathing suits. When we get outside, my aunt stops me before I can run off.

"Winnow, this is Andrea. She works with me," my aunt says, pointing with her lips to a stout woman with long blonde hair wearing a black one piece bathing suit.

The suit had bright pink flowers and a pink ruffle at the waist that made it look like she was a retired, unkempt ballet dancer.

"Hi," I said, as politely as I could without seeming inconvenienced.

The woman looks me over, and says, "Oh my god, you're skinny." She takes a puff off of a long white cigarette, and says, "You make me sick." She does a fake shiver, like the sight of me was so repulsive it shook her to the core.

I didn't say anything, just stood there.

My aunt didn't say anything either, except to ask the woman for a drag of her cigarrette. The woman took one more drag, her face contorted in disgust, before handing it to my aunt and blowing the smoke in my face for emphasis.

"You're smoking?" I ask my aunt with surprise, who had, as far as I had known, given it up years ago.

"I'm an adult, I can smoke if I want to," she says. The statement made sense, but her motivation did not.

I walk away from them, a little less excited to get in the water. I couldn't help but think that my aunt was changing somehow.

It had only been little things, but now it seemed like all of the little things were piling up. It was like a there was a dam between my aunt and everything else. Was this what gramma meant when she talked about movements becoming things? What was my aunt holding onto? What was this dam made of?

I sit on the edge of the pool, and try to think of what it is about her that has changed.

And then it occurs to me that my aunt has stopped being brave. Even when she had boyfriends in the past, and she would feel self-doubtful, she would still try to do what was good for her in some way, whatever way she could see to do, whatever way that wasn't being blocked by her obsession with that guy.

But now, it was like she had slowly surrendered all of her ability to care about herself, and had allowed bad magic to paint over her face and skin. She was trying her best to leave her broken self behind, refusing to be vulnerable.

About a half an hour later, I ask my aunt if I can go home. I tell her I'm not feeling good.

I stop in front of Jim's house on my way home. I notice that his garage is open, and his car is gone. I decide to jump on his trampoline while he's away, as I had restrained myself from the activity thus far.

It takes only a few minutes of jumping before I am feeling the resurgence of joy in my body, my desire to feel good, and alive.

I fall onto my butt, and slowly come to a still.

I lie back on the trampoline and spread my arms over-head. The sky is such a bright blue. It reminds me of a story my grandmother told me about the blue sky.

Blue Bird Calls in the Day

Blue Bird was singing one morning, welcoming in the day with much excitement. He stopped when he heard a noise. It was Cardinal. He was snickering at Blue Bird.

"What's so funny?" Blue Bird asked, happily, as Blue Bird enjoys funny things.

"You're funny, Blue Bird," Cardinal says.

"What do you mean?" Blue Bird asks, unaware he had made a joke.

"The way you sing for everyone to hear," Cardinal says, looking around for the other animals. "Aren't you embarrassed to sing your love song so loudly?"

This upset Blue Bird tremendously, for he thought of Cardinal as an older brother. He looked up to Cardinal.

"Maybe he's right," Blue Bird said to himself, after Cardinal had flown away.

The next morning, Blue Bird sat in his tree, depressed. He really loved to sing with the morning sky kissing his feathers.

But he just sat there.

Blue Bird was so unhappy and cornered by his thoughts that he didn't even notice the sun was stuck at the horizon.

As the hours passed, the animals gathered in the field to look with surprise and confusion at the sun that had not yet risen.

Another day goes by, and more animals gather, becoming fearful.

"How will I hunt at night if there is no night?" Owl asks.

"How will we drink the nectar of the flowers if they do not open with the afternoon sun?" the small flying creatures ask.

On what should have been the third day, the animals notice that Blue Bird is missing.

"Where is Blue Bird?" they ask.

"He is sulking in his tree," Cardinal says with a nervous glance, knowing he had upset Blue Bird, but not wanting to admit it.

Coyote, who is feeling less of a trickster now that he, too, is fearful that the sun may never rise, goes off with great concern to find Blue Bird.

"Hey, Blue Bird!" Coyote shouts when he reaches Blue Bird's tree.

Blue Bird is sitting with his head tucked into his feathers.

Coyote's eyes widen large when he sees that Blue Bird is much more blue than he has ever been. He is radiating blue.

Coyote grins.

"Hey Blue Bird, how about a song?" Coyote says.

Blue Bird says from tucked feathers, "I don't feel like singing today."

"Of course you do, Blue Bird!" Coyote says.

Coyote thinks for a minute, then says, "If you sing, I promise the whole forest will dance to your song."

Blue Bird sits in his tree, thinking about what to do, "I don't know," Blue Bird says.

"You will know if you stop thinking about what you know." Coyote says.

Blue Bird looks up, and sees that all of the animals have gathered around his tree, including Cardinal, who is now looking afraid for Blue Bird.

Poor Cardinal, Blue Bird thinks. *He looks so afraid. What is he afraid of?* Blue Bird feels courage and love swelling within him. *I will sing a song for Cardinal,* he decides. *I will show him how easy it is to sing for love.*

Blue Bird opens his beak, and his song floods the forest, blue light shining from the bottom of his heart, which is as deep as the sky itself.

Slowly, the sky is filled with blue, raising the sun like a boat on the water.

The whole forest dances, the animals sing their own songs of love and appreciation for the day that gives them their ways.

Even Cardinal can be heard singing. It is a sad song, but it is true, and it is good.

I lie on my back. I think about my grandmother. She's always been the kindest, most true person I've ever known. She has the widest, deepest heart, that when you found yourself in it, you actually found yourself in it. She would never, ever try to take or make you give up any part of your self that you needed to be full. Gramma said that people who took from others what they thought they needed to be fuller were looking away from the fullness that was their own for some reason.

Maybe my aunt has had enough of her fullness, and is trying hard to be less than full. What parts of her fullness are so hard to deal with that she thinks it's better to create a smaller, modified version of herself for others to connect to her through? Is fullness seen as a threat to the adults she chooses to spend time with?

I knew my aunt had been married before when she was young. She told me that she had two miscarriages before the age of twenty-five, and that her husband gave up on his ideas of making a family with her.

Ever since then, my aunt has felt like something was missing. Like she was less of a woman because she hadn't any children of her own. I could tell she had great swaths of painful color she wrapped herself in, like a sad shawl dancer, dancing for judgmental men, begging them to score her a woman. And she has been seeking the approval of men ever since. And it's gotten worse. She's lost or given up most of her confidence and self love over the years.

Who is Jim to tell my aunt what's good for her? He's just a creep. I wish she'd be brave and listen to her sad skin. A sad song that is true is better than one that is absent or untrue.

I miss my gramma so much. And my momma. And my dad. And my sister. And my aunt.

I try my best to be full with my own beautiful tragedy that is feeling more and more vulnerable to the carelessness of my aunt and the onslaught of her friends.

Still lying on the trampoline, I lift my head at the sound of a door creaking somewhere nearby. I look around, but can't tell where the sound had come from.

I lie my head back down and close my eyes, letting my face warm in the hot afternoon sun.

A loud *clunk!* Jerks me up again. I prop myself up on my elbows, and this time I scan the neighborhood much more carefully.

All is quiet and still.

Everyone is at the pool.

And then I see movement in the doorway of the small toolshed just to my left.

It is Jim. He is standing a foot or two inside of the shed, his face in the shadows.

He is staring at me. And his pants are pulled down enough so I can see the top half of his boner.

He is rubbing himself.

He looks down to his penis, then to me.

I stare at him for a few seconds, then look away and lie my head back down, resting my hands on my belly.

I'm not sure why, but my reaction is mostly one of indifference. I'm not frightened, although my heart is racing, and I am only slightly aroused.

It's more like I saw him "doing his thing," acknowledged it, and just want to go on about my way.

I understand myself to be a sexual being, and was not upset to see him as one, just a bit surprised at how he had chosen to show me.

Honestly, seeing him like that felt better than having him hint at that part of himself covered up in a conversation.

In that shed, he was vulnerable, alone with his feelings in a small hiding spot.

He reminded me of me.

The sun became unbearable, and I walked home, with a secret skip in my step.

I didn't see Jim around much after that. He avoided me like the plague. He must've started telling my aunt to leave me behind, because that's exactly what she did. He couldn't face the sexual part of himself, and he couldn't face *me*. And he got my aunt to look at me as little as possible, too.

My aunt started to stream onto me all of the storywaters she had thrown from her skin in her attempts to shape her identity into one that was pleasing to Jim.

She started making me do things she knew I hated, and denied me of what I enjoyed.

My afternoons at the pool were the first to go, even though we had almost a month left paid for.

Apparently, I had become the face of everything she looked upon in an unholy light inside of herself, because she started dropping me off at church by myself on the weekends. She told me *I* needed divine guidance. *I* was a sinner. *I* needed to be saved.

I think she wasn't willing to admit to Jim all of the things that I knew about, and every one of her last boyfriends knew about. She thought that the things she could see inside of her were responsible for men turning away from her. I wish she would just sit with those ugly things so they could unfold as beautiful, eternal things that flow through us all. But she refused to see them, and had bundled herself up in superstitious control of her skin.

6

FOR THE LOVE OF GOD

S ATURDAY WAS A STUDY group and on Sundays there were three hours of service.

When I rebelled and my aunt found out I had skipped church service to play at an elementary school playground nearby, she made me also go to the Wednesday study groups, which were held in the evenings at the homes of congregation members.

I hated study group days, until I found a way to make a game out of it.

Every Wednesday, I would excuse myself from the dozen other people who also attended, and lock myself in the bathroom to masturbate.

It was fun to dig around for interesting things to rub myself with. I never stuck anything inside of my body, unless it was the size of a pencil, but I stopped using pencils when I found out how much it burns if you rub wood on yourself for too long. I imagined the pencils catching fire from the flaming heat of my tinder bits. And I wasn't sure they couldn't.

I had long ago learned to avoid rubbing myself with things like soaps and whatnot, after I had masturbated with my sisters roll-on deodorant when I was eight and ended up with a bladder infection. The doctor had pressed against my bare belly with gloved hands, and asked me, "Does this feel funny?" and I had giggled because I had a secret no one knew, but nodded my head yes to indicate that the giggle was from his touch and not my secret.

I also thought it was fun to see how long I could masturbate in other people's bathrooms before someone would come to check on me.

When I would come out and take my seat, I would spend the rest of the time looking around at the other people, who would have either curious looks or looks of concern. "Was I feeling okay?" "What was I doing in there?" For the love of God, I wished that someone would just come out and ask me, so I could tell them the truth, and see the looks on all of their faces.

I imagined some of them would giggle and choke on their own breath, while others would pretend they didn't hear, or else get up and walk out, with or without cursing in their exit.

I had especially wished someone would have asked me that during the one study session where masturbation was brought up, and the literature bull crap we were supposed to have read, studied, agreed with, and then preached, said that you should refrain from masturbation because God has a plan to bring someone special into your life, and that masturbation robs both you and your partner of the godly, Christian pleasure of sex after marriage.

I say bull shit. I've heard my aunt talking to Andrea about a CNA where she works. She says that the wife cries to her on a weekly basis over the fact that she has not once had an orgasm, in her *entire life,* and she questions whether or not that means her husband is the man she's meant to be with.

Can you imagine? Marrying the man of your dreams, only to have to come to terms with the fact that the logic of your religious, superstitious beliefs and that of your heart do not comply? Something has to break. Pick your poison. Love or religion.

My aunt stopped making me go to study groups when she noticed I was coming home amused. She didn't know what I had been doing, and didn't ask, but I figure enjoyment was not what she was hoping I would get out of the activity.

Soon after, she insisted I cut my hair.

My hair had never been shorter than mid-back length, but I agreed to let her cut it to my shoulders, after she had gone on about how cute it would look.

When I realized she was actually cutting it just an inch or two long, I yelled at her and locked myself in the bathroom. I stared in the mirror and cried, knowing I'd have to let her cut the rest of it that short.

After that, I distanced myself from her, and began not wanting to come out of my room or get out of bed.

One day, I could hear Andrea telling her that I was lazy, and to just wait until I was a teenager.

I cared deeply for my aunt, but I gave up on having not only a relationship with her, but with myself as well, after her friend cornered me one day, and told me how disgusting I was. I asked her what she meant, and she said, "I know about you. You're a lesbian."

I was so confused, and upset.

I asked my aunt what her friend meant by that, and my aunt said, "I know you had a girlfriend. Sarrah's mom told me that Sarrah *like* liked you, and that she saw the two of you kissing."

Once again, my private world was being turned upside down, this time to be shaken out and laughed at for what came tumbling out.

"Why did you tell her that? She's saying mean things to me," I cried, pleading with her to show me some compassion.

"Well, you should have thought about that before you decided to go and be gay."

"I didn't decide to be anything!" I shouted at her.

She slapped me hard on the mouth, one of her rings chipping my front tooth.

I could taste blood in my mouth. I covered my lip and ran to my bedroom.

That was it for me.

I felt totally alone, unwanted, and completely misunderstood. I started to develop "an attitude". Everything that was communicated between my aunt and I had near-bursting emotion behind it that I didn't know what to do with.

I got my first period at school not long after that, but didn't bother telling my aunt until she questioned me about why her pads were missing. I reluctantly told her.

For a moment, it looked like something other than destructive forces were moving inside her, but then it passed, and she said steely, "What am I supposed to do now? You're going to pay me back for those," like the pads were the one thing I was to be held accountable for.

I realized then that I was actually being held account-able for the insecurity my aunt felt about me becoming a woman and her unhealthy concept of what a woman should be.

7

TWELVE AND A HALF DEAD

I STARE DOWN AT the doorknob. It had been painted brown but the paint is wearing off and the copper underneath has begun to tarnish in the spots that see the most wear.

I see myself in that doorknob, metaphorically speaking. I've spent the last few months struggling to surface from beneath the whitewash I've had splashed upon my face, and across the sensitivity of my skin, only to have my true colors tarnish at the surface because I don't know how to care for them properly.

I slump my sweaty forehead against the door. I don't have the strength or the desire to be vulnerable anymore. I feel like any moment now, I might pick up a paintbrush and commit against myself the very acts that I have fought against—the redrawing of my identity to include only the *things* that my aunt and society tells me is acceptable. The things you hold onto when you're afraid of being moved and changed by the storywaters.

The pretty brown paint of the doorknob is eternal in its image with re-application, just like the unmessy face I feel I am required to put on for the world. But the changing skin of the copper underneath tells a story that must be listened to and understood if it is to be in its best shape.

I look intently at the tarnished copper. I can't help but think about the effort put forth to cover such a thing up, and wonder, why not just learn how to take care of the copper itself? I feel a churning of hate for the world that has been built around me. The world, that as I grow older, closes in on me in imposition, demanding I recreate the moldings I have inherited. I slowly click the button, locking the bathroom door, and turn to face the mirror.

I touch my face. It is uneven from the inclement, hormonal storms of adolescence. I have come to know my skin as a tender, sore place in every form of its expression. I close my eyes and gently run my fingers over my eyelids. They are puffy after shedding many tears over the course of the last four hours since my aunt left for work and I was supposed to leave for school.

I open my eyes.

I hug myself and tell myself I'm sorry. I don't know what else to do. I don't want to be like them. I don't want to uphold sterile standards of life.

I can feel my stories creeping in to comfort me, but with a motion of my mind, I clear them away. I do not want to carry their vulnerability with me anymore. I feel like I will try to tear it apart if I allow myself access to it.

I unscrew the lid of the fist-sized bottle. I count the contents. There are twenty-eight round, white pills.

I hope that's enough.

I draw water from the running faucet with my hand, and swallow them one by one.

Each one feels like a prayer for peace. Each one a curse upon a masking structure.

I lay down on the floor.

I feel like I've been cleared out on the inside. I'm so broken. I'm done crying. Tears don't help anything.

I feel powerful for the first time in I don't know how long. I feel in control. And less afraid.

I don't know what will happen as the minutes and hours pass by now, but I know that if I surface on the other side of this storm alive, I would rather be a forgettable void where things go to fall apart than be left in charge of creating good things.

I have become familiar with how things fall apart. And where there is familiarity, comfortability is within reach. The creation of good things, however, seems like a fairy tale that breeds an untrue concept of free love and familial togetherness.

I take the time to say goodbye to the parts of myself that I have found to exist in other people who have helped me over the years. I embrace them, and then let them go. I am saying good bye. Maybe for forever.

I curl up in a ball and hug my knees into my chest. I think about the last year of my life as I fall asleep.

I wake up and turn to lie on my side, the flesh underneath me a deep red after hours of stillness.

My flesh feels so weak.

But I don't care.

I sit up.

I pick up the empty bottle of pills and bury it under the
trash in the waste basket.

I don't want my aunt to know anything about what I
do anymore.

I don't want her to know that I feel like I don't want
to be here anymore, alive.

I throw up, and lay back down.

I close my eyes and wait for the darkness to carry me
away.

8
GOING HOME

"**W**INNOW!" I CAN HEAR my aunt pounding on the bathroom door in the distance.

My head is pounding both hard and light. My body feels weightless, my blood weak. I reach up to turn the light on, and slip in my own vomit, falling to my knee hard.

God dammit. I realize that my attempt to take my own life had failed. Now I have to deal with my aunt. But now, I really don't care.

"Winnow! Open the door!" my aunt says, frantically.

I turn the light on, and open the door.

My aunt looks at me, "What the hell happened to you? You look like shit."

"I don't feel good. I threw up," I tell her.

"No shit." She looks around at the both fresh and dried vomit on the floor. "Holy shit," she says, and slumps down in the hallway and begins to sob.

"I'm okay," I tell her.

She looks up at me, and I can tell that it is more than the sight of me that has shaken her deep.

"Gramma died," she says.

The blood that was left moving in my veins rushes far and fast away from my head, "What?" I say.

"Gramma's dead," she says through her tears. "She died last night." She looks at me again, "I tried to call you from work. Your great aunt called me on my cell, I was trying to tell you to pack up. We're going to Red Lake. Tomorrow. "

I sink down to the floor and hug my aunt. We hold each other and cry.

It took us two days to get to Red Lake. During our drive, my aunt had to pull over a lot, as I was throwing up white foam every few hours.

My aunt, in her weakened state, became sympathetic towards me, and did her best to comfort me.

I didn't tell her what I had done. Something inside of me had shifted. I was willing to hurt myself to escape my feelings. And I didn't care if I was alone

Somewhere between Texas and Minnesota, I snuck away to a mail drop box at a grocery store while my aunt used the restroom.

I opened the metal door, and gave the letter I had written to my gramma a kiss. I knew she would never read it, but it made me feel better to ask her things that maybe I'd get the answers to someday, somehow.

I reread the address on the envelope, and wondered if I was crazy:

To my dead grandmother,
wherever you might be.
Or anyone with a dead grandmother,
like me.
The return address just said:
Winnow Sticks
Lost
Red Lake Reservation, MN

I drop the envelope into the slot, and look around to see if anyone saw me kiss the thing. Just a dad with two kids was looking at me, smiling. I smiled back.

The last few hours before we reached the rez, I was feeling much more nauseated and weakened than I had all day.

I became light-headed, and fainted for a few minutes. When I woke, we were in Bemidji at a gas station. My aunt was shaking me.

"Winnow! Winnow, wake up!" she saying, frightened.

I looked down, and saw that I had peed my pants.

"Oh my god, what's the matter with you?"

"I don't know," I said.

But I knew.

It was my parents. I was afraid to see them.

My aunt bought me a ginger ale, and told me it would make me feel better. It did, a little bit.

When we got to the rez line, I started to cry. "Auntie, I'm scared to see my mom and dad," I confessed.

"They're probably scared to see you, too, Win."

My great aunt had said that everyone was in Red Lake at my gramma's wake, including my parents. My dad flew in from California. My mom from Nebraska. They had arrived at the Bemidji airport the morning after my gramma died. I hadn't talked to them on the phone. I was too sick the first day they called. The day after that, I pretended to not be feeling well enough because I was afraid I would just cry the whole time. I missed them, but I was so angry at them for abandoning us. I thought if I talked to them I would tell them I loved them, and then tell them I hated them. I didn't have the stomach for that. I wasn't even sure I had a stomach anymore.

Auntie and I pull up to Gramma's house. I recognize my Great Aunt Bernice's old car. My Aunt Bernice moved in with Gramma after Gramma fell and broke a wrist last winter. I can see signs of her presence in the marigolds and daisies lining the house. My great aunt loves marigolds and daisies. Gramma is more a fan of wildflowers. I think they look nice. I'm sure Gramma did, too.

It's about 2 a.m., and the late summer air is thick and moist. Crickets are chirping in the wood line, wood frogs sing in the pond behind the house, and my ears hear the familiar sound of mosquitoes. Thousands of them.

I am tired and weak, but I feel relief. I am home.

I wrap myself in my yellow and white knitted shawl my aunt had made for me the first year we were together, and walk into the house.

My Great Uncle Ned is asleep in a living room recliner. A cigarette butt burns nearby. I recognize two of my cousins sleeping on the couch and floor.

My uncle wakes up. He and my aunt talk for a while. My aunt tells me that more of my relatives are at the community center where my grandmother's body is being looked after. She asks me if I want to go over there with her. I do.

We pull up to the community center, a small fire burns outside. Two men sit nearby, poking at it with sticks, letting out big belly laughs every now and then. I recognize one of the men to be another of my great uncles. Gramma had four brothers. Two of them still lived here, in Red Lake.

I step out of my aunt's pickup truck. My skin is pale and clammy, but I feel ready to face my parents.

We go inside the center, where a few old ladies are gabbing in Anishinaabemowin. I can't understand what they are saying, but they sound serious.

I look around. No sister. No parents.

I walk over to my grandmother's casket.

I pull my shawl closer around me.

I look down at her body. There's something missing. What I'm looking at doesn't quite seem like my grandmother. I wonder where the rest of her is.

I close my eyes, and let my knowledge of her wrap around me, hugging me, "Hi gramma," I say, "I'm back."

I reach down and touch her arm.

I think about how supportive and accepting she was in life. She was always encouraging people to try new things, and work on things they enjoyed. Gramma showed me how to bake. She said I was a natural. The only thing I've baked since I moved away is frozen pizza.

"Look who it is!"

I turn around to see my sister Maggie. She's tall and skinny, her brown hair in two french braids. She's wearing a red half-shirt, short jean shorts, and sandals. Her arms are outstretched.

I run to her and squeeze her as hard as my arms can manage. I cry loudly.

"Aw, I miss her too," she says, hugging me back.

"Where's Mom and Dad?" I ask.

She looks at me with a painful, scared look in her eye, "Winnow, they left earlier today."

I sink to my knees, and sob even louder.

"Why did they leave us?" I pull at the back of my head, crushing my body together, into a tight ball. "Where did they go?" I ask, after puddling out across the floor, my body rid of tears and sharp sorrow.

"Well, you'll never believe this, but they left *together*. Yup. Mom and Dad are back together. Who knows for how long, though. They left for Nebraska, to where Mom lives. They told me to give you this." She digs into the pocket of her shorts, and pulls out a wad of money. "Eight hundred, I counted. They gave me some, too."

The money didn't make anything feel better.

I wish I had ramma back. She'd know what to do.

"I'll be back," my sister says when she see's a guy come into the center. They leave the building together.

I lay on the floor in front of my gramma's casket. I wipe the snot from my lip. One of Gramma's old lady friends walks over to me.

"You're Winnow, aren't cha?" she says. She has dyed black hair that is short and in tight curls, just the way gramma wore hers.

"This is for you," she tells me, handing me a zebra-striped, velvety photo-album-style book.

"Thank you," I tell her. She walks back over to her friends.

I look at the book closely. It's soft, and has little beaded flowers here and there on the cover. I open it up to see what look like recipes. There are no photos, except at the very back there is a picture of me and Gramma, baking. I must've been two years old, and was standing on a stool so I could help Gramma knead dough. We were both covered in flour, and we were smiling at each other.

I close the book and hold it close to my heart.

I wake up, feeling like new, and pull off the jacket someone must have covered me with. I don't remember falling asleep. My aunt sits nearby, cradling a coffee cup in both hands. She nods her head empathetically at my Great Aunt Bernice. They are about the same age, these women.

"Come here Winnow," Aunt Shelly says to me, patting the bench beside her.

I sit by the women. Aunt Shelly offers me coffee. I shake my head no. I still prefer cocoa or tea to coffee.

"So, Aunt Bernice wants to know if we're going to be staying with her at Gramma's house, back-a-town."

"Winnow can stay with me," Maggie says, walking towards us.

With those words, I feel the world expanding. I have options.

Maggie isn't quite fifteen, but she's lived on her own with her boyfriend Travis for almost a year. Gramma tried her best to keep Maggie at home, but around here, girls grow up young. My gramma got tired of fighting with her.

Travis is eighteen now. They live in Redby, which is a village about five miles from the village of Red Lake. Both are on the Red Lake reservation, along with the other villages of Ponemah and Little Rock. There's also West End, Barton's, Circle Pines, and some families living here and there within the borders of the reservation.

Maggie and Travis have a roommate, Devon, who is also eighteen. The house is in Devon's name. His mother passed away, leaving it to him, her only child.

My aunts share a look of concern.

"I dunno, Winnow," my Aunt Shelly says. But the loss of gramma had weakened her desperate grip to control things, to control *me*, and she added, "You'd have to go to school," she said with conviction.

I hadn't thought about not going to school. I nod my head yes quickly, and say, "I would go to school, I like school."

"Easy there," my sister says and laughs, "you're going to make me look bad."

"You keep that dirty Devon away from her. She's just a baby," my aunt says, patting me on the head.

I make my grinch face, and scrunch up my shoulders under her tutelage.

"She's not a baby, Shelly, you're just an old lady, is all," my sister retorts on my behalf.

My aunt swats at her from across the table, Maggie easily moves out of her reach. The three of them laugh.

Maggie to the rescue! I think to myself. I feel my body start to relax. No parents? I'm a little scared, but I'm not looking back.

A few minutes later, I'm hugging my aunts goodbye.

"Funeral's at eleven," my great aunt says.

I nod my head in acknowledgment.

I follow Maggie outside. It's about six in the morning. Half of the sky is painted a medium blue, the other is orange and pink. The pine trees are still dark. They sway in the wind, their movement reviving a presence inside of me that I haven't felt since I was a little girl, welcoming me home.

I breathe them in, welcoming them home, too.

I wrap my shawl under my chin, and skip behind my sister.

"Cut it out, dork," she tells me.

My skip evaporates with my joy, leaving an "adult" posture of seriousness in its place. My walk slows to almost a halt when I realize I don't know my sister any more.

"Get in," she tells me, as she gets into the front passenger seat.

I go to open the nearest rear door, and see through the darkly-tinted window, a guy shaking his head no, and giving me the "other side" sign with his thumb.

I slowly walk around the back of the car. I knew my sister lived with people, but for whatever selfish, childish reason, I was expecting it to just be me and her.

I get in the other side and slide onto the red, faux leather seat.

My sister turns around to face me. "You wanna get high?" she asks me.

"What do you mean?" I ask.

The driver, presumably Travis, chuckles.

"How old are you, ten?" the guy in the backseat next to me asks.

My sister sees my confusion, and offers, "You know, smoke weed."

"Oh. Okay," I say, trying to sound casual. I hadn't smoked weed before, but knew that most of the older people did. I hadn't thought about it in years; my aunt doesn't smoke weed.

"Gimme twenty bucks," my sister says.

I just look at her.

"For the weed," she says.

I dig the money wad out of my little sequenced purple purse that I had begged my aunt for. It was only fifty cents at a second hand store, but I swear she acted like I was asking for something hot off of the runway.

"Moneybags!" the guy next to me says excitedly, "Fuck yeah, let's party!"

The guy next to me is good-looking. He's darker skinned than me, and has big brown eyes and a defined brow. His hair is short under his white basketball cap.

I get excited. I had never partied before. My aunt had made sure of that.

"Winnow, that's Devon. And you know Travis, right?" my sister asks.

I had never met Travis, but I nod my head yes.

"Geez, it's only 6:15. The liquor stores aren't open for a few hours," my sister says.

"Let's go to B-Town and get some grub before they open," Devon says.

"B-Town?" I ask.

They all laugh at me.

"Bemidji, dork," my sister says, rolling her eyes.

"I'll buy breakfast," I say. What else was there to do with the money?

We get to a 24-hour restaurant. My sister and Travis sit on one side of a booth. Devon gets in on the other before me, as I am shying away from the whole, eating-in-public situation, per usual.

Instead of scooting in, Devon stays on the outside edge of the bench, pats his knee, and says, "Take your seat, young lady." He and Travis laugh.

My sister says, "Ick, push over Devon," and grabs me by the sleeve of my shirt, pulling me down to sit.

The waitress brings us menus, and I feel panic take hold of me.

"I'm not really hungry," I say, even though I am, and have money to buy anything I want on the menu. My nerves are wringing my stomach out, telling it to keep empty.

"Whatever, skin and bones," Maggie says. "You're having pancakes, and bacon, and," we both start laughing.

"So, are you a virg?" my sister asks, when I'm halfway through my French toast.

"A what?" I ask, wiping syrup from my lips with my sleeve.

"A virgin," she says. "Aunt Shelly thinks you're not. She thinks you had sex with her boyfriend, Jim."

My fork drops, "What? No way! That guy was a weirdo!" I didn't feel comfortable enough to tell her about what he had done in the shed that day.

"Yeah right, you look like you've done it before," Devon says.

I'm taken aback by how straightforward they are. I've never been talked to in such a way before.

"It's okay, Winnow, just because aunt Shelly is a tight-puss doesn't mean you have to be. You're with me now." She pauses to look me in the eyes. "Just tell us. Have you ever done it? With a guy, I mean?" She winks at me.

"Oh! She's a lezzie," Travis says, "Hikes, Devon."

Devon punches him in the arm, "Nah, shut up."

I try to avoid eye contact with them.

I've never had sex with a guy before. In fact, I had never even kissed a guy, and I was starting to feel like a little kid. I realize that I have the opportunity to step into the role of someone with more experience than I actually have. I had tried to kill myself, and failed. What was lying about who I was going to do? Obviously, they didn't care about the truth anyway.

"Okay, I'm not a virgin," I say, "but I've only done it once."

"Close enough," Devon says. I can't tell if he thinks it's a good or bad thing.

After breakfast, we stop by a house on the way to the beach. Maggie goes inside, and comes out just moments later, "Score," she says, and we drive off.

We go down to the water front, and Maggie pulls out a sandwich bag with weed in it. She pulls a folded up piece of paper from her back pocket, and unfolds it. She cuts the weed on it with a little pair of scissors I give her from my purse. The scissors look like a crane. Gramma sent me them on my eleventh birthday after we reminisced over the phone about the time I had put on a play for her with a pair just like them when I was little.

"Travis, gimme a paper," she says. I wonder if the paper she already has isn't good for some reason.

Travis hands her a small, rectangular piece of paper that she uses to roll the weed in. I realize that there is more than one kind of paper at work here. She licks it shut.

"Damn, girl," Travis says, "save some of that tongue for me."

Maggie gives him an amused look.

"Girl knows how to use her tongue!" Travis says loudly.

"You sure don't," Maggie says.

"Daaammn!" Devon chuckles, "Hikes," he says.

We stay at the beach until the liquor stores open.

"What do you want?" Travis says.

"I dunno," I say.

"Do you like sweet drinks?" He asks.

"I dunno," I say again, "probably."

"Get her some wine spritzers," my sister says, "She's probably a light weight."

"Hey, I weigh 108 lbs!" I say in protest. It took me a long time to get past 100. For a while, I wasn't sure if I was going to make it.

They all laugh at me again.

I hand Travis a hundred dollar bill.

"Just get whatever, then?" he asks me through the car window.

"Yeah, whatever you guys want," I say.

Travis comes back with a box full of different sized bottles in one arm, and a box of beer in the other.

"Hell yeah!" Devon says.

My sister pops the trunk and Travis puts everything except one of the bottles in the back.

We start to drive back to Red Lake, and Travis hands my sister the bottle. She opens it, takes a drink, and passes it to me. I take the lid off, and sniff it. My arms and legs shudder at the smell of it.

"Drink up," she says.

"What is it?" I ask.

"Whiskey," Travis says.

I take a small sip. My belly tightens, my nose and throat feel like they're on fire. I try to hand it to Devon, who pushes it back towards me and says, "Chug it up first, then."

Against my body's wishes, I do what I think "chugging" it means.

"Atta girl," Devon says, taking the bottle from me.

We drive around for a while, drinking, and at about 10 o'clock, I remember that gramma's funeral is at 11.

"Oh shit!" I feel distress wash over me, "Gramma's funeral!"

"That's tomorrow. Chill out, you're going to kill my buzz," Maggie says.

We get back to their house in Redby. My sister takes me into the basement, where a quarter of it has been cleared out for my stuff, I assume.

"We'll try to find a curtain to hang up," Maggie says. "Keep all these pervy men out."

I wasn't convinced that a curtain would keep any real perverts out.

I only had a couple of drinks from the bottle of whiskey, but I was feeling like I could say anything. I didn't have my normal anxious feeling. I munched on chips and candy like a fat kid.

Maggie turns a stereo on loud, playing rap tunes I hadn't heard before.

She starts dancing, and gets Travis to dance with her.

"Come sit by me," Devon says.

I do. I smile shyly, when he puts his arm around me, and pulls me into his chest.

He smells like clean laundry and weed. I lay my head on his chest, and reach my hand up to feel it. I giggle.

"What?" he asks, looking down at me.

"Nothing," I say.

"No, what is it?" he asks.

"You make me horny," I tell him.

He laughs, and says, "Good."

"Hey," he says, pulling my chin up to his face. He kisses me. His lips feel soft and full, so does his tongue.

"Mm," he says, "you're making me horny, too."

"Hey, pervs," Maggie says, handing Devon a cup filled with ice, and what I assume is whiskey and cola.

Devon takes a drink, and then brings it up to my lips so I can take a drink, too. He kisses me again, and this time he tastes sweeter. I wonder if I do, too.

I feel like my sexuality is coming out of the toy chest I had kept it in. It is being opened up and provided a gusty, lusty wind to set sail on. Full speed ahead to who knows where?

I get nervous, and pull away from him, "I have to pee," I tell him.

He pulls on my arm as I try to escape to the bathroom.

I sit, peeing. Maggie comes in, handing me a bottle of something green.

"Try this," she says.

I take a drink, and smack my lips, "What is it?" I ask.

"Pretty tasty, huh?" she says.

"I dunno," I say, feeling a bit nauseous.

"Gimme that," she says, and takes it from me. "Don't forget to wipe," she says, leaving the bathroom.

I sit on the toilet, feeling like a fraud. I've never had sex before. Why did I say that I had? If I have sex with Devon, won't he know that I'm a virgin? Won't I bleed everywhere? That's what I hear happens the first time. I sit and try to think hard about anything that could have de-virginized me over the years.

I tried using tampons once. They were slim ones, for young girls. I got them from a dispenser in the locker room at school. They were really uncomfortable, and I stopped using them after not knowing any better, or better yet, not having any common sense, I tried sticking two in at once. Well, it was more like I stuck a second one in without pulling out the first. I was in between classes, and thought I didn't have time to clean myself up, so I tried putting a second one in, and it went in fine. It wasn't until at least a full day later that I remembered I had never taken out the first one. I had to dig around in there a little to find the string. When I pulled it out, the top of it was green, I shit you not. That scared me. Never used tampons since, but always wondered if they can make it so you're not a "true" virgin anymore if you use them when you've never had sex.

I stick my fingers down there, feeling for some sign of a "cherry." I'm not sure what I'm looking for. For all I know, my cherry could have popped on that tree that I fell on when I was four. That was a horrible experience.

I was wearing a dress, tights, and dress shoes. I don't remember what the occasion was, but the attire wasn't what I was used to. I was used to shorts and no shirt or shoes. That's what you wear, if you're a kid on the rez climbing trees.

There was a favorite tree I liked to climb in gramma's back yard. It had arms that were thick and went out just as much as they did up.

My dad yelled at me, when he saw me trying to get up the base in my dress shoes.

"Winnow, get down from there!" he had shouted, "You're going to fall!"

I got down. But Dad was busy chopping wood, and my four-year-old mind was busy forgetting what he had just said.

I climbed up that tree again, getting up far enough to be passed the main fork that had a jagged stump of a branch as big around as my leg that stuck out about five or six inches.

Everything went black when the pain hit. I just remember hearing myself scream like a wild cat.

I could barely walk for days, but I could stand. I stood on the back porch, holding onto the railing, imagining my legs doing what I knew they were meant to do.

"Oh, you can walk," one of my older relatives had said with disgust when they found me at the railing, before grumpily shutting the door between us.

I had a large, black bruise down there, and Dad was upset, and said he didn't want to take me to the hospital because they would accuse him of doing bad things to me. And Mom said she didn't want me to go through the same humiliation she had experienced more than once when she had to have a male doctor look at her girl parts.

Ever since then, I have wondered if I would be able to have children. And whether or not that tree took my virginity that day.

Now, as I sit, drunk, I want to find out.

I open one of the drawers under the sink, and find a metal bottle half full of cheap perfume. There is a long, white, round cap on it, and between the cap and the bottle, it is about the size I imagine a boner would be.

I try to fit it inside me, and I feel a small amount of pain. I don't get it in very far, just enough to get passed the opening.

I pull the bottle out, and to my surprise, there is a tiny amount of blood on the cap.

Damn.

Does that mean I'm not a virgin anymore? Did I seriously just pop my own cherry? How lame is that?

I feel like I have just denied myself an experience. Like I have bypassed something. My lies are dragging my experience along by the ears, and somewhere in the hurry is my identity. I was pushing myself ahead, trying to be what? Get where? I didn't know, and I was pretty numb to caring. If my new family wanted me to play a certain role, I was fine with painting myself into it for their entertainment. It was better than trying to build something that I cared about that could just be torn down without any say about its destruction.

I stand up, and have to lean on the sink. I quickly drop to my knees, and turn to the toilet to throw up.

I wash my face with cold water, and let the water run over my hands.

I go back into the living room, where they are smoking another joint. My sister passes it to me, but I decline, and say, "I think I need to go to bed."

"I told you she was a light weight," Maggie says to Travis, who just nods.

"Bed? The party's just getting started," Devon says, grabbing at my waist to try and pull me onto his lap.

I maneuver out of his grip, "Really, I just threw up," I say.

"Go ta bed then, jeez," Maggie says, and holds her arms out wide, an invitation for a hug.

I hug her weakly, and she kisses me on the cheek, getting pot smoke in my eye from the joint in her hand.

"There should be a blanket down there for you. And a pillow, too," she says.

I am asleep before I have time to cover myself.

In the morning, I wake with a terrible headache. My body feels achy, too. I have never blacked out before, but now I understand what grown-ups mean when they say that.

My legs feel weak. I become afraid. Did Devon rape me? He wouldn't do that, would he? Now that I had popped my own cherry, it would be hard to tell, now, wouldn't it?

"It's just a hangover," Maggie says, in a grouchy tone. "Devon tried to sneak downstairs with you last night, but I told him to get the hell out of there."

She opens her eyes wider, lifting her head up slightly from her pillow, "What time is it?" she asks.

"Almost ten," I tell her.

"We better get ready," she says. "Hand me a smoke, would ja?" she says, pointing at a pack of cigarettes next to me on the floor. "Want one?" she asks me.

I shake my head no. Some adult things could wait. The smell of her second hand smoke was giving me a pretty good idea of what it was like, anyway.

A lot of people attended Gramma's funeral. I recognized less than half, but my Aunt Shelly told me we're related to most of them.

"I've missed you," Aunt Shelly says to me, giving me a hug. "Jesus Christ, you smell terrible. Have you been drinking? Smoking?" She looks at me with big, wide eyes.

I don't say anything, just lean into her.

"Spend the night with me. It's lonely over there with just that old lady to talk to," she says. We have a giggle.

"Okay," I say. I could use a bit of familiarity after the night I had.

I hold her hand, and we walk out to the burial site together.

9

THIRTEEN

"**C**OME OUT TO THE casino to pick me up tonight," Maggie tells me, "I miss you."

I had only seen Maggie a couple of times a week since the funeral. I missed her too. I had told her that I felt bad for our aunties, and felt like it was up to me to try and cheer them up. I didn't tell her that the real reason was that I just didn't want to be around her and those boys. But after almost a year of being back on the reservation, partying with her and Travis and Devon wasn't any worse than what's been happening to me after school in back-a-town.

Some of the boys that live near Gramma's started harassing me when I go for walks in the neighborhood.

First, they were just whistling at me and hollering sexual things when I'd walk by the house they'd all hang out at.

Not long after, they stopped me on the path that runs in the ditch, and asked me if I had a cigarette. I told them no. Then one of them asked me if I wanted to get high. I said no. Then one of them asked me if I wanted to get poonged by a big you-know-what. I laughed, and said no, but he must have taken my laughter to mean that I was actually interested, and he put his arms around me from behind. I tried to wiggle away, but he was strong. He put me in a choke hold, and I passed out and woke up just moments later, and he was holding me up with his hands on my boobs, squeezing them. I was light-headed and disoriented. I swatted at him and stormed out of the ditch to cross the street. "She likes it!" He had said, loud enough so I could hear. His friends all laughed.

Ever since then, they have called me a "tease", and a couple of months ago, the four of them surrounded me, and tried to pick me up and carry me off into the woods that fill a good area in back of town behind my Gramma's house. Two of them had my arms, and two tried to grab my feet. I kicked one of them in the balls. He fell to his knees, and the others laughed at him.

I didn't know what they thought they were going to do or get away with, but once they had me in the tree line, they surrounded me and started groping me and sticking their hands under my clothes, pushing me further into the shadowy understory. I knew I wouldn't be able to fight them, and I was afraid of what they might do to me if I tried.

I was preparing myself mentally for a horribly intrusive experience, when someone called to them from the porch of a house not far away. Two of them ran quickly to the caller, while the other two continued with their effort to debase me, until they, too, were drawn off by the loud, booming voice of a someone no doubt meaner and louder than they.

I had tried to tell my aunt that I didn't want to walk to school anymore, but when she asked why, and I said, "The boys are trying to..."

She had interrupted me right away with, "You're going to get on birth control. I don't need any more kids running around. And don't try to blame boys for you wanting to have sex. I don't care if you want to have sex, but you had better be on birth control first."

And that was that. And she meant it. She picked me up from school the next day and drove me straight to the clinic, where they stuck my butt cheek with a needle. Once every three months, the doctor said, I'd have to have a shot to avoid getting pregnant. I said I could just not have sex or avoid being raped to not get pregnant. My aunt didn't think that was funny. I hadn't meant it to be funny.

Since then, I've just been laying around the house with no desire to get out and do anything. It felt safer, not doing anything. But I knew I had to do something at some point.

So, it was with some relief, that I told Maggie, yes, I'd ride with to pick her up.

"Come stay with me, too," she said.

There was a pause.

"Okay," I told her. I was actually kind of excited. I knew that I would more than likely end up having sex with Devon if I moved in with her, and living with someone you can have sex with? That was like a fantasy of mine since I was eleven.

She said it was going to be Travis and Devon that I'd be riding along with, but when it was time to go, it was just Devon that showed up and honked the horn.

"Where's Travis?" I ask as I get in.

"Selling weed," Devon says.

We drive for about a half hour with the windows down. It reminds me of when Dad would take us out hunting. We'd be out all night, us kids in the backseat, taking turns singing to the classic rock songs on the radio, claiming it wasn't fair when someone else got to sing to our favorite song. Then singing along anyway and getting yelled at by the kid whose turn it was supposed to be.

We'd get stuck out in the woods every once in a while and have to walk for miles in the morning after spending the night in the car with a few dozen mosquitoes. Mosquitoes are hard to kill in the dark.

We'd come home all bit up, scruffy and hungry, and mom would listen to our story and tell us how worried she was, but that she knew we were all right, because our dad was good at finding his way out of the woods. Then Gramma would make us too many pancakes and send us out to play.

"Where are we?" I ask, as the car comes to a stop along the side of the dirt road.

"The river road," Devon says, taking a swig from his beer can. He tosses the empty can out the window, and reaches into the backseat for a new one. He grabs me one, too. I accept, and take a drink.

The new night air is dark and muggy. The sounds of the wetlands in the late spring are truly incredible. The calls of the frogs and insects are so intense that I feel like I can slip off out onto the wind with them, as if my recognition of who I am was being opened up to include a new dimension on the frog wind.

"What are we doing here?" I ask him, becoming nervous when he shuts the car off and takes the keys out of the ignition.

"You know what we're doing out here," he says, trying to sound sensual, but succeeding only at raising the hair on my arms in alarm.

"Aren't we supposed to pick Maggie up soon?" I ask, hoping that commitment will supersede any plans he had to try and have sex with me. I mean, I wanted to have sex with him *at some time*, but I was starting to think that I'd never actually feel ready to do it.

"Not for a couple of hours," he says.

I had no idea we left with so much time to spend together. Alone. What was Maggie thinking? Did she know Devon was going to be like this? Did she care?

"You ready to get schooled, or what?" he asks me, grabbing my knees and pulling me towards him, spreading my legs.

"What does that mean?" I say, trying to keep words and thoughts between us.

He chuckles and says, "It means you've got a lot to learn, little girl."

I can't explain why his outright behavior was turning me on, other than it was calling out to my own animalistic drives.

"I can show you," he says, pushing his hand up my thigh to my chest.

I knew he could. But I didn't feel ready. I guess I was hoping for some sort of romance leading up to the event. I expected he put some effort into coaxing my sexuality out. But it felt like he was trying to break in. Maybe that's all he knew how to do. Maybe that was the summation of his "schooling"; how to break and how to get broken.

I decided it was better to bend than to break. If I decided to do it even though I wasn't ready, at least I'd feel in control. So I gave in to him. And it was exciting, awkward, virgin sex.

When we finally made it out to the casino, Maggie got in the back seat, took one look at the two of us, and busted out in laughter, "Fuckin' pervs!" she said. I guess it was that obvious what we had done.

10
FOURTEEN

Overfull

I had been sexually assaulted a handful of times since the age of twelve.

The last time happened when I was walking to my gramma's house from the grocery store just after dark.

I was visiting my aunts, and we had spent the day together baking, eating, them drinking wine, me sneaking a glass here and there, and listening to Minnesota Public Radio. It had been a good day, until then.

I had gone to get some confectioners sugar, as we were still just baking away into the night. A car stopped beside me, and two guys I knew from school asked me if I wanted a ride. I told them no, that I lived just a few houses down.

The one in the passenger seat got out of the car quick, saying, "We're not asking," and before I could think to back away, he was next to me, and he was holding a golf club.

He was dropping the head of the club to the ground by his foot. That weakened me. It reminded me of my dad telling me where to stand when he wanted to control my behavior. He motioned with his chin, and said, "Get in."

For three hours, they took turns driving and holding me captive in the back seat. The one next to me putting their arm across me to keep me in the car while they switched spots.

They had a hammer that looked like it was made for smashing meat, because it was spiky on the part that you hit stuff with. I was told that I would die if I didn't do things with them.

I cried and begged them to stop when they had pulled over and were both in the back seat with me.

I couldn't give in anymore, and refused to have sex with them at the same time. One of them got really mad that I wasn't doing what he wanted me to do, and was hollering at me, saying, "Look away! I can't kill people that are looking at me!" as he held the hammer above my head. I had my hands up in horror, trying to block myself from him.

I begged the lesser angry of the two to tell him to stop. He didn't say anything except, "Better do what he says."

They had dropped me off at my gramma's, saying, "You better not tell anyone," to which, I had acted tough and told them I wasn't going to say anything. Who was I going to tell?

This was just one of the many abuses I had suffered at the hands of careless men. The pain, anxiety, and my dissociation from the cause of these things had been steadily building over the years, and after this happened, I tried to make it fit into the teaching, good-flowing pain that I knew. But it had become too much. This pain really did break me.

My insides had finally been gutted and spilled out, the whole mess heavily fertilized with the magic of mean-spirited men. I suffered from overexposure; I became infected. What could grow from such a mess?

My aunts were sleeping in recliners when I got back. I fell asleep outside on the porch, staring up at the stars, wondering how far my pain and fear stretched out beyond my body. It felt like it was traveling to at least the edge of the solar system. But all distances are hard to measure when you lose your sense of judgment. When you've given up on subtle, sensitive tools shaped in the current of the unknown and replace them with hard pounding ones designed to control the flows that cross the skin. It becomes impossible to see, feel, or hear the signs that tell you how far you are from home, from safety. How far you are from caring. And it becomes near impossible to find your way back.

There were oceans of storywater running through me from that great black sky and into the beyond. In my attempts to protect myself, I had gradually destroyed the natural places where it was supposed to stream out of and into my life. I didn't cry. My flesh had forgotten how. I had forgotten how to gather myself. I felt broken, my inner light scattered and distant as the stars in the sky.

I sat on that porch for hours, looking into the emptiness of my surface. I finally realized the damage I had done, in my apathetic shrugging off of my inner witness. I had forgotten how to listen in earnest.

What would my hands, ears, and tongue be used for, now that they were no longer interpreting the storywaters clearly? I remember what gramma had said about how people teach themselves to use these tools to do unnatural things in the name of escaping fullness.

I was starting to understand what she had meant.

When you tell yourself you don't matter, you don't care if you hurt, if you die, if people use you; you're teaching yourself ways to frame things with self-destruction in mind, creating tools that are constructions to this end.

One of these tools is a voice that is created to allow the shredding of tender skin connections to be seen and felt as a source of power, control, and stature.

That voice is at the hub of a subculture that crops up in places where it's easier to give up and be in control of the bad things happening to you. It's the, I-Don't-Give-A-Fuck culture.

IDGAF is written on bathroom walls, fogged school bus windows, and the faces and skin of lots of people of all ages around here.

People harden, and act like they are proud to not G-A-F. Like this behavior is some kind of asset or currency.

But living with this voice is like living inside a torture chamber that barely keeps you alive and feeding on your own suffering.

How do you find your way out of this masochistic hell hole? How do you tell the butcher that what he is selling is a part of himself that he desperately needs?

People stuck in the IDGAF mindset would rather gnash their teeth and stick their finger up at someone, anyone, like a weapon displaying their quickness to cut, than to try and build something with them requiring tending and care.

Impatience is a keystone of the culture. Vulnerable conversation is limited. Hateful, bitter, fighting-for-control language however, is in ample supply. Quiet moments are lost to anything loud enough to distract from the begging of tenderness to be rekindled.

Adults yell and cuss at their children, calling them mean names like they have no feelings. And the children are just as angry, and are learning to stop listening at an early age.

I found that the IDGAF voice prompts IDGAF actions. You don't have to think much when your brain is programmed for self destruction. Everything new looks like an old enemy. There is no spontaneous or steady observation of emerging beauty. There is only a massive knot of fear, anger, despair, and separation, fuel for the IDGAF machine.

From my broken state, I reprogrammed my tools to circumvent natural emotional response, to connect to an idea center where I store false truths about why things happen.

I tried to put the pieces of my broken, internal landscape back together. But I was afraid. So afraid. I couldn't make sense out of the enormous waves of pain and fear.

Putting my landscape together again produced a grotesque forging of my identity, as I tried my hardest to leave my broken girlhood out of my awareness. I began to hate femininity, and see it as a weakness inside of myself. I wanted to feel more powerful, and started to copy behaviors I believed strength emanated from. I took cues from men who had never integrated that wild, peaceful discipline I looked to as a girl into their lives, but had instead come to believe that masculinity meant domination and control over the feminine.

I started to engage in anything to keep me distracted from the true and tender darkness begging to be held, sang. The darkness where wounds sink in to throb, to heal. The place where mystery drums up my heartbeat. The epicenter of my femininity. The river of a thousand foot steps, heavy in their eternal journey became frantic, feared sounds of self-told, non-truths. My heartbeat became a ghost in my body. Its presence something vague and to fear.

I started to look for, and expect pain everywhere. Even when there is no real threat, I find what I am looking for. When you feel like you have too much pain and fear, these things spill out and fill up everything outside of you, and try to get back in, to be held as a part of you. This is why I feel afraid and suffer when everything should be okay; large quantities of my pain and fear are stuck on the outside of my skin and I feel like I am under attack non-stop.

I feel so weak. I want so bad to change things. I'm just not sure where to start.

FIFTEEN

IT'S EARLY MORNING. I am woken by the song of the robin that ends with a sound so fantastic it must spin worlds awake.

The disparity between that song and the one suffocating my insides is crushing.

I don't care, I don't care, I don't care—
that's the song.
The repetitive hum of TROUBLE!
mind an body follow blindly along,
by defeated necks and genitals,
by hair, kicking and screaming,
to the mantra, "I don't care about anything,"
in a voice so blatantly disbelieving.
Trustful trying has long since departed.
In its stead a lust for lying grins,
to smother feint hearts barely started.
The tears never come.
with tensions ever high;
no rest for the weary
in mad suicide.

The hum in the room
is all that is left,
where humanity struggled
to connect the dots,
insanity deflects.

Somewhere between that robin and me, the world drops off into a deep, deep gorge, dry as bones. From the bottom, I stare upwards towards the wet sky of the robin, thirsty for a song that is true to fall ever so far and land upon my lips.

I look around the room without picking my head up. Beer cans and liquor bottles are strewn about. There are people passed out on couches, the floor. Fear rises within me, and explodes outward of my skin. It permeates this scene and I am unable or unwilling to move. The two have become inseparable.

I feel both physically and mentally ill. But I know that today will be just like yesterday. There's no stopping this downward spiral now. This dry digging of a massive, shared grave.

I scan my body, my mind. Paired with my fear is a disinterest towards life and experiencing new things.

It feels like all of the nerve endings in my body have been short circuited after too much stress, and I am now wired into this life that is really no life but a repetitive sorrow.

I've been living with Maggie, Travis, and Devon for two years now. We drink a lot, smoke a lot of weed, and

Devon and I have an arrangement: free rent as long as I have sex with him.

Of course, it wasn't negotiated as plainly as that. He says I'm his girl, even though I know he has sex with other girls. I've decided I can live with that. I've never thought of him as some true love or anything. Not that I'd know what true love is anyway. True love, bare-boned love; is there even a difference? I rationalize that at least he's not violent towards me, like some of the other guys on the rez.

I've started writing a lot, filling up at least twenty notebooks with poetry and drawings. My notebooks have been the one safe space I have, where I can talk about what's going on with me, where I can explore for myself, how I feel about things.

In my writing, I've begun calling out into the universe for help. I ask for help from whoever is out there, listening. The kinds of conversations I had kept in my heart, I've started writing. I need help learning how not to feel like that anymore. I don't want to feel all that pain trapped inside of me anymore.

After asking for help, I was visited by spirit of a plant. A corn plant. One morning at dawn, as I lay in my bed, dreaming, a corn woman came to me and took me away from my body and brought me into her own. I entered her as she stood growing in a field. I could feel the power in her form, the energy she was being given by the sun, so bright. I felt the strength in her connection to the earth; so grounded. And she was full of love.

I woke up from this dream, so overwhelmed by this experience of something outside of the pain I knew. I was overjoyed with tears; I ran out of my room, excited to tell anyone who would listen about what I had just experienced.

I had experienced hope.

12

SIXTEEN

MY GRAMMA USED TO say that there is more understanding and responsibility with each added drop of water to a flow.

Now, as I sit in the canoe my grandfather left behind nearly thirty years before, I find myself humbled by the gatherer of the waters keeping me and this old boat in buoyant perspective.

Amik, the beaver, appears from below to demonstrate how to identify, allow, and care for my own gatherers of flow with patience, steady persistence, forgiveness, and the taking of small enjoyments in the process of opening wider channels.

Simple things like opening up a moment to relax into the sounds of birds on a summer wind have recently proven to offer more than the promise of self-destruction, now that I am practicing the art of "what-is".

"What-is" is what I call the true presence of things that exists in movements unaltered by my mental filters, and the observation of such things in their unaltered state. It also describes participation in such things.

It may sound absurd, but I am literally retraining myself to see, hear, and feel things for what they are.

My newly regrowing tools gather and focus the substance running through our shared landscape. It is an intentional, surrendering motion, to be led by the flow and its ever changing and widening collection of opportunities to be ever more full.

Watching amik these last few weeks in the relative silence of the wetlands, I have learned that the task of the patient isn't to shape, but to support the water. The thing about water is that it *wants* to find more of itself, like it recognizes the goodness in being an ever bigger whole, and I find my own movement drawn onward by this same gathering bond.

After leaving the IDGAF life style behind, I attempted to avoid the destructive behavior of other people and spent the first five months in the basement of my gramma's house, trying to shut the world out. I thought if I separated myself from the world outside for long enough, I would heal naturally.

That didn't work as I had hoped.

I found that when you do nothing, your brain and body replay everything you've *already* done in an attempt to communicate with the passage of time. This kept the IDGAF voice alive and well, as I wasn't cultivating any new, enlivening experiences to open into.

One morning, or afternoon or night, I was never really sure what time of day it was, for the dungeon has no window to the outside world, my aunt pounded on the door, and when I didn't get up to answer, she mumbled about leaving something outside of it.

It was my gramma's recipe book. I had forgotten all about it. I had kissed it like it was Gramma's head, and told her thank you. I would return to it sometime, and then I tucked the book away in a sock drawer in an upstairs bedroom.

As I studied it and my response to it, it seemed to be free of bad magic. There was nothing scary about it. In fact, it seemed to hold promise. My heart took a deep inhale of IDGAF-free air, and exhaled a sense of grounding that I had not had since I was a young girl.

Something took notice of this break in the momentum of my torment.

How did I do that?

Could I make the relief last longer?

Could I stop feeling like this?

I remember taking a moment to just feel.

There was an awful churning inside of me, a nasty storm of voices and mean-spirited chatter. And while I've always known it's not me, I can't seem to get rid of its influence.

It feels like my life is a rolling ball of self-hating, habitual momentum. It is huge and its movement great.

It spins with massive, forced truths and undigested trauma. It's a great big poopball of self defeat.

I sat in that basement, feeling paralyzed by its monumental horror. Until it occurred to me that if I could see and feel it, I must be able to touch it, effect it, slow it down. I knew that seeing beyond it was out of the question for the time being, as it must be so big because it needed lots of tending to. But I just knew that something different, something beautiful, something *real* was out there, beyond it.

I made up my mind then to do whatever and go wherever I needed to, to find out. To try.

I took my grandma's book, and left the dungeon behind.

I went looking in search of a real movement. I've now spent a few months camping in the woods and along the shores of small waters within a days walking distance of my gramma's house.

In paying attention to the simple, quiet, wild things, I have slowly reduced the spin of the confusion and fear inside of me.

The feel of things—everything—is a lot different without cookie cutters on my brain.

I think often about how I arrived to where I am today. I thought about all the superstitions about men and women I'd heard over the years. I was never taught how to see through the magic and superstition. They don't teach that in the tenth grade. But they ought to.

I would go to that school.

Unexplored emerging character, vibrancy. Full of *knowing*. That is what life is like when it's not being ran through mental and emotional storywater filters that pick things out of the water—the *ugliest* of things—to hold onto and try to share.

I feel like I've finally returned to the advice of my gramma after all these years; returned to my *listening in*. I still have uncontrollable anxiety and fear sometimes, but I'm also starting to experience life as a force that listens back. And loves.

I see now that the "perfect" shape of love can be designed by each individual person and get stuck in their story flow, making them think they have love when in fact they are picking and choosing what they want love to be, and hating other people for not reciprocating their vision.

But love is a river.

There are no cookie cutters in the shape of love. It is a shape ever growing, ever enlarging. Ever redefining, like the river of one long story mother, depositing new sediments of form for the next mother and the next to hold and then to set free downstream.

I reach under the seat of the canoe for my leather bag, and pull out a notebook, pen, and lighter.

My name is Winnow Sticks,
and I come from the I-Don't-Give-a-F**k Reservation
of American Indians.

Our reservation crosses the borders
of state and mind.
It holds in bondage people of color,
women people, children people,
born into poverty blind.
It surrounds us when we're at your front door.
So sleep well, unafraid,
of losing face or space.
We are stuck on our insides,
our identities hazed.
And although we may have Indian names,
we don't know we're real.

I crumple the page and then light fire to the wad. I place it onto the surface of the still pond.

"Gramma, I miss you," I speak aloud to the fire. Gramma was the fire in my life that burned with care.

"How do I make a fire like yours, Gramma?" I say, the ashes of my pain lightly floating away with the wind.

The wind blows over my skin, turning up leaves in my emotional landscape, such that in their dance they tell me what I already know but seems like the task of a lifetime: you have to care.

How do you care all the time?

I take a few minutes to trace out that which I felt connected to by a thread of care.

"I care about animals. And children."

Another wind blows another message across my skin: you have to care about yourself.

Myself?

A tear forms in my eye. I slump down in my seat, "But I don't care about myself. Not really." Right as the words leave my mouth, I identify the voice speaking them to be the ghost of my IDGAF past.

How could I be so devoted to change and still feel this way?

I close my eyes and sit in silence, witnessing the rolling ghost ball of apathy as it spins and grinds against my current will to change, to care. I realize that I am doing everything I can. I realize that I am the only one here to witness this process, and that I am the only one capable of being okay with the fact that it could take years of doing just this to turn my life around.

I close my eyes and smile.

I am more than okay with that. I *am* that.

Author's Note

Thank you for picking up and reading this book, presumably to the end, which was in fact, a beginning.

A lot of what happens in this book did happen in some shape or form in my life. Most of the characters in this story were inspired by real people but fictionalized enough to provide privacy.

A little about me, I don't have a sister named Maggie. I grew up with two brothers, and later, two stepbrothers and one half brother mostly in Minnesota and always knowing Red Lake to be home. Like Winnow, my parents divorced when I was nine. I moved to Kansas and then Arkansas with my mother before returning home to Minnesota to live with my father and step-mother at the age of thirteen.

The voice of Winnow's grandmother is inspired by my paternal great-grandmother, a career cook and baker who worked for the Red Lake school district, as well as the voice of a grandmother I found within myself on my path of healing.

The short story "Blue Bird Calls in the Day" was given to me after I offered some asemaa and prayed for a story to include in this book that would illustrate the challenges Winnow faced and the courage she would need on her healing journey —my journey. I wrote the story down almost word for word as I heard it told to me in my mind shortly after prayer.

A lot has happened since I first wrote this book. Since 2015, I have published a cookbook, a middle grade illustrated book, and brought the character Winnow back for a happily ever after in the contemporary romance *Native Love Jams.*

Native Love Jams is currently in the works to be a feature-length film.

I live in Duluth, MN with my husband and son, where I am currently finishing a new sci-fi rom com novel and planning the next.

KEEP IN TOUCH

tashiahart.com
realnativeromance.com
tashiamariehart@gmail.com
IG: @tashiahart
facebook.com/tashia.hart.5